THAT'S MY GIRL

JILL ROSS KLEVIN

SCHOLASTIC BOOK SERVICES
New York Toronto London Auckland Sydney Tokyo

ISBN 0-590-31274-X

12 11 10 9 8 7 6 5 4 3 2 1   2   0 1 2 3 4 5/8

THAT'S MY GIRL

A Wildfire Book

CHAPTER
ONE

Becky awoke to the jangle of the alarm in her ear. She opened one eye, closed it, and burrowed back under the covers. A quarter to five. An uncivilized hour! No one ever got up at a quarter to five A.M. That wasn't morning. It was still the middle of the night.

She swung her legs over the side of the bed and sat there listening to her body. It didn't sound too good. The calf muscle she had strained during yesterday's lesson throbbed painfully, and her spine felt as though it had been taken apart vertebra by vertebra and put back together again the wrong way around. If she felt this bad now, in the middle of the week, what kind of shape was she going to be in for the weekend?

Groggily she staggered down the hall to the bathroom. On a sliding scale of one-to-ten, she would rate this a zero-minus morning. Some mornings were better than others. She had five mornings, six mornings, occasionally a seven or even an eight; but let's face it, when you had to get up at a quarter to five, *no* morning was ever that great. One thing she promised herself. Someday when she was rich and famous, she was going to sleep every day until noon. Then all her mornings would be ten-pluses.

She showered, brushed her teeth, ran a comb through her hair, and headed back to her bedroom. She gazed longingly at her bed. It looked so cozy and inviting standing there, the patchwork quilt thrown back to show the pretty blue-and-white ruffled sheets; the afghan her mother had crocheted for her folded neatly over the curlicued iron footboard; the pleated bedskirt and pillow sham in the same fabric as the sheets. The sheets matched the windowshades, the curtains, the wallpaper, the rocker pads, and even the porcelain picture frames her mother had hand-painted herself. The room was the creation of that talented interior designer/fashion expert, Sara Bacall, otherwise known as Becky's mother. She had done everything in it herself, even the wallpapering and the carpentry. When it came to doing anything creative, especially with her hands, she was a whizz — unlike Becky, the *klutz* of the universe, who couldn't even hammer a nail into a wall without destroying at least one finger in the process.

Becky made her bed and got into her practice things. She crossed the room to the ballet bar to start her morning warmup, beginning with a series of bends and stretches to limber up. She watched herself in the mirrors to make sure she was doing it right; that she didn't cheat, slump, sag, or favor the bad leg. Those mirrors were her nemesis. You couldn't get away with a thing with all those mirrors around. It was kind of like having Vera standing guard twenty-four hours a day, watching every move you made, coming down hard on you if you slipped and made a wrong one.

When she had been younger, she had had to do her exercising down in the basement, a dark, damp, smelly place that was full of weird noises she had been convinced were ghosts. Then, just before her twelfth birthday, her parents had built this addition on to her room. They had lined the walls with mirrors, covered the floor with a plush, white carpet, and hung up a ballet bar and a sign: BECKY'S GYM. Even doing a lot of the work themselves, it had cost them a fortune. It was so typical of them to blow that money on her, rather than on themselves — that trip to Europe they had been planning since the beginning of time, a new car to replace the decrepit, old Volvo, a new roof for the house, new clothes, new furniture. Well, *she* would do it all for them someday when she

3

was rich and famous. If things went as planned, that would be soon.

She lifted her leg up on to the bar, sliding it out as far as it would go until she was practically doing a split standing up. The calf muscle felt as though it was being squeezed in a vise, but she kept on stretching. That was the only way to work out a muscle spasm, but wow, did it hurt!

"You're only getting what you deserve, lazy!" she scolded the scowling girl in the mirror. It just went to prove that when it came to muscles, Vera knew what she was talking about. The night before, when Becky had been leaving the rink after her lesson, Vera had come charging out after her.

"Go home. Take a hot bath. Rub linament into ze leg, den wrap it, und vear voolen legg varmersz to bed!"

"Yes, Vera," Becky had replied meekly. Then she had gone home, bolted her dinner, taken a fast shower, and fallen into bed, too exhausted to do another thing.

"Ouch!" The muscle knotted into a cramp. She took the leg down from the ballet bar and began to massage it. Let's face it, she was no masochist. She didn't go *looking* for pain. But she *was* a skater, and pain came with the territory, like funny-looking feet, chronic backache, over-developed leg muscles, and chapped hands. She shook the leg out a few times and when the spasm had loosened, put it back up on the bar and started the stretches over again. "That's my girl,"

she mumbled to herself, her eyes locked determinedly with those of the girl in the mirror, "stretch." Up close the girl's eyes were *lapiz* blue, a nice color if you happened to like prosaic, old blue eyes. They gazed steadily back at her, the irises narrowing to pinpoints in the light.

"You sure don't look like a superstar, Becky Bacall," she murmured. That just went to prove how little looks had to do with superstardom. Looks weren't the essential ingredient. *Talent* was. Plus drive, self-discipline, dedication, training, and endless hard work. Beauty was *not* a prerequisite. Take Dorothy Hamill, for instance. She was no sex goddess-movie star, but she *was* one of the three or four top girl figure skaters in the world, and if Dorothy Hamill had done it, Becky Bacall could too, and *would* in the next winter Olympics.

To skate in the Olympics, that had been her dream ever since she could remember. Rebecca Victoria Bacall, unextraordinary sixteen-year-old girl from Northridge, Long Island, with her picture on the cover of *Time*; her own TV special; hosts of adoring fans clamoring for her autograph; manufacturers begging her to endorse their products.

Of course, if you were going to be on TV and have your picture plastered all over magazines and shampoo bottles, it helped to be pretty. She wasn't, at least *she* didn't think so. She looked just like her father. As her mother said, they had one face. It was a nice enough face, appealing, winsome, pert maybe, but definitely not pretty. The mouth was too wide, the nose too snubbed — a typical girl-next-door nose, complete with freckles. Overall it was just too ordinary and bland. The eyes were okay. "Expressive eyes," some sportswriter had written in an article about her for *Newsday*. They were deep blue and had long, long lashes and little laugh wrinkles at the corners. Her father, the poet laureate of Northridge, was always spouting corny sayings: "The eyes are the mirrors of the soul." In her case, it was true. Anytime anyone wanted to know what she was thinking, all they had to do was look in her eyes.

It was weird sometimes looking so exactly like someone else, even if the someone *was* your father. Aside from the color of their hair (his was light brown; hers, blonde like her mother's), they were identical. They even had the same smile, a quick, engaging, and very toothy smile that lit up their faces and crinkled up the corners of their eyes. Becky made sure to smile a lot. Smiling showed off her teeth, which were terrific. People were always saying, "Wow, have you got terrific teeth!" Jed had once asked if she had seventy instead of the standard, regulation thirty-two, and Dee was always saying she was the only girl in the world with a boyfriend who got turned on by teeth instead of other, more provocative parts.

The thing she liked best about herself was her hair. It was blonde and thick and wavy, and she wore it long, hanging all the way down her back, except when she was working out and she braided it or put it up on top of her head. A lot of skaters wore their hair short, because it was so much easier and more practical, but no matter what anyone said to try to convince her, she refused to cut off even one fraction of an inch. With short hair she would have looked just like everyone else. With long hair she was unique, special.

She took the bad leg down from the bar and put up the other one. If she had to say so herself, she had a pretty good figure. What figure skater didn't? She was one of the few skaters who was tall, five-foot-seven and still growing. She was thin, but she had big bones, broad shoulders, long legs, and no hips or butt whatsoever. People sometimes wondered, with her size and build, how she managed to be so light and graceful. She couldn't account for it. Maybe it had to do with weight distribution.

She finished the stretches, then did some side bends from the waist before taking the leg down from the bar. Her mother stuck her head in the door and said, "Good morning, lovey. How's the leg? Any better?"

"Uh, uh. If anything, worse. Guess I should've listened to Vera."

"Should I put the hydroculater up to boil?"

"No, Mom. No time. I'm late already."

"Okay. Breakfast in ten minutes." Her mother sailed off down the hall, whistling Chopin. Becky got down on the floor to do her situps. One of the things she loved about her mother was she wasn't one of those "smother mothers." She never laid the old "I-told-you-so" trip on you, the "If-you'd-listened-to-me, this-never-would-have-happened" routine. She was strict about some things — keeping your room neat, eating nutritious meals, helping with the housework, being responsible —but she believed in independence and self-sufficiency, so, in general, she gave you a chance to make your own decisions and do things for yourself. She was there for you if you needed her, but she didn't crowd you or invade your private space.

Becky fell back on the carpet with a groan. This sure was one of her rottener mornings. If she had known what it was going to be like being a skater, would she have stuck to ballet, or become a cheerleader instead?

The answer to that was easy. A talent was something you were born with, something you owed it to yourself to develop, no matter how difficult it was. And it *was* difficult. Sometimes you asked yourself, *"Who needs this?"* But you knew who. *You!* Let's face it, as difficult as it was sometimes, you knew in your heart you never would have chosen to go any other route. Skating was what you were born to do, the thing you loved doing better than anything else in the world. And, no matter how hard it was, or what you had to give up along the way, you knew someday it was all going to be worth it, someday when you skated in the Olympics and won that gold medal.

CHAPTER TWO

Becky limped into the kitchen. Her mother was laying strips of bacon on the griddle to fry.

"Would the future world's champion mind pouring the orange juice and starting the coffee? The future world's champion's *mother* is up to her elbows in bacon and eggs."

Becky got out the orange juice and glasses. "Mom, it's positively intimidating how you manage to look like that at six o'clock in the morning. Couldn't you at least have the common courtesy to be a little puffy around the eyes?"

Her mother laughed. "Can *I* help it if I'm age-less?"

At forty her mother looked more like thirty. She had this absolutely unbeatable combination of attributes: great skin, good hair, fabulous bones, muscle tone, and no wrinkles. Her face wasn't exactly pretty. More like attractive. Big, green eyes, an aquiline nose, a beautiful, sexy mouth, and the world's highest cheekbones. Her hair was blonde, like Becky's, but it was straight, and she wore it real short, cropped close to her head like a boy's. Everyone said the style really suited her. Her body was still great. She even still looked good in a bikini. Of course, she had this misguided idea she was overweight, which was ridiculous. She was only overweight if you compared the way she looked now, at forty, with the way she had looked when, a scrawny girl of fourteen, she had been a sectional champion on her way to the Nationals. She rarely skated anymore. Even after all these years, skating still made her nervous. She did work out in a gym, though.

Becky watched her mother turn the strips of bacon. "Gosh, that smells good! But I'd better not have any. Every time I eat bacon, I get a stomachache." She took her vitamins down from the shelf, shook out two C capsules, a high-potency multivitamin, an iron tablet, and an E, and started popping them into her mouth one by one, washing them down with orange juice. She heard footsteps in the hall, and her father staggered in. He was the last person in the world you expected to see at six o'clock in the morning. He wasn't a morning person. He'd sleep every day until noon if he could.

"Daddy, is that *you* behind all that hair? Wake up, Daddy. It's morning!"

"No, it's not. You can't fool me." He shuffled over to the table and fell into a chair. He had a phobia about going for haircuts, so most of the time he walked around looking like a shaggy sheepdog in need of a grooming. He was more the cute type than the handsome type, with his sleepy, blue eyes and snub nose. The thing she liked best was his cleft chin, but that wasn't visible these days. He was growing a beard. So far it looked pretty scruffy.

"It's unhealthy to get up at this unearthly hour. It's indecent!" he groaned, blinking up at her.

"What are you doing up, Daddy?"

"I'm flying to Boston this morning to talk to the A.M.I. people about that printing job."

"But, Daddy, I thought you said you wouldn't work for them. You said it was against your principles."

"Principles don't pay grocery bills," her mother put in, taking the bacon from the pan and spreading it on a paper towel on the countertop.

"But, Mom, you're the one who's always saying people shouldn't sacrifice principles for money. Anyone can have money, even a crook, but there are too few people around with principles. Daddy," Becky said, turning to her father, "do you want strawberry jam on your English muffin or orange marmalade?"

"Orange marmalade, Beanie, and for fifteen

thousand dollars I guess I can manage to repress a few principles. Fifteen thousand will pay for a lot of skating lessons."

She started to protest, then decided to drop it. But how come the first thing either of them ever thought about, in any given situation, was her? How come he hadn't said, "Fifteen thousand will look pretty nifty in our savings account," or "Fifteen thousand will pay for a great vacation for your mom and me"? It was a heavy responsibility when your parents focused with such a vengeance on you all the time — always so intent on what you were doing, on your future, making all these huge sacrifices on your behalf. It made you feel you had to live up to all their expectations; that if you didn't, they'd be destroyed, and it would be all your fault.

She glanced up. Her father was surveying her with a worried expression. "Am I imagining it, or have you lost weight?"

"You're imagining it, Daddy."

"Skinny. Pale as a ghost. Big rings under your eyes. What kind of life is that for a young girl, spending all your time at a damp, cold skating rink overtaxing yourself?"

"Here we go again, folks!" Becky stuffed the last bite of muffin into her mouth, grabbed her plate and fork, and stood up.

"You ought to be going out, having fun, enjoying your youth while you can," he said. "Isn't that what being young is all about?"

"Not for me!"

"Alex, leave her alone," her mother whispered. "She does it because it makes her happy."

"*Happy?* That you call happy? Okay, skate, but don't give your whole life up for skating. I'm not saying she ought to give it up; just slow down a little. Take some time for other things . . ."

"Daddy, has it ever occurred to you that those other things *you're* so keen on may not appeal to *me?*" She dumped the plate and fork in the sink so they clattered on the porcelain, making him cringe. It wasn't that she didn't appreciate his concern, or that she would have wanted him to care less about her; it was just that he was so out of touch with what she was all about. She was one kind of person; he wanted her to be another — a giddy, giggly, bubble-headed teenager with tons of friends, who spent all her time running around having what he called *fun.*

"Daddy, I can't change into someone else just to make you happy," she said.

"Change into someone else? Who ever said I wanted you to change into someone else?" he said in a wounded tone.

Becky started to reply. "We have to go," her mother put in, giving her a warning look behind her father's back. "Alex, what time does your plane leave?"

"Ten-fifty."

"Oh! I'll have to do the cleaning up later."

"No, I'll do it!" He jumped up and started stacking dishes up his arm, the way he had done when he'd been a waiter at summer camp umpteen years before. She headed for the door. He stopped stacking and started after her. "Haven't you forgotten something?"

They met halfway between the door and the kitchen table, not such an awfully romantic locale for a love scene. The kiss wasn't exactly what most people would have expected from an old, married couple of eighteen years, but then they never did anything like an old, married couple. It was comforting having parents who liked one another so much. As long as you had to go through life an only child, at least you knew that, no matter what happened, it was always going to be the three of you.

"You taste delicious," her mother said, turning to go. "Like bacon and marmalade."

Becky gathered up her things and followed her out the door. "Well, 'bye, 'bye, Rudy Valentino," she called back over her shoulder. "Good luck in Boston."

CHAPTER
THREE

Becky dumped her things in the back and climbed into the passenger seat beside her mother. "Too bad I don't have my driver's license yet. You'd be able to sleep in the morning."

"And how would I do that?"

"I'd drive myself to the rink, of course."

"Oh!" Her mother pulled out of the driveway, heading toward town. "And what do you propose I do all day long, stuck in the house without my car, hmmm? Take in laundry? No, I've gotten used to getting up in the middle of the night. I may even be addicted to it by now. I'd probably have dreadful withdrawal symptoms if I couldn't do it anymore." She pulled up at the stop sign at Main and Maple, shot across Maple onto Marlboro, then stepped on the gas so the Volvo could make it up Marlboro Hill. The poor, old thing wheezed and coughed, complaining audibly all the way to Tain Drive, where it sputtered and nearly died, then revived enough to make the turn onto Vista with trepidation.

"Come on, baby. You can do it. Do it for Mama," Becky's mother urged, moving her foot up and down on the accelerator. "Every day I wonder if we're going to make it. Every time we do, I'm amazed."

"That's Maggie Mayhew," Becky said as they pulled up at the rink entrance, and a small girl in a red snowsuit dashed in front of the car. "She's eight, but you ought to see her skate. Vera says she's going to be another Elaine Zayak."

"That's your competition? Undersized eight-year-olds?" her mother sighed. "They're making them younger and younger."

"I know," Becky sighed, suddenly apprehensive. "I'm practically over the hill right now."

"Well, you'll still be the youngest member of the Olympic figure skating team next year." Her mother switched off the ignition, settled back in her seat, and began idly twisting the fringed ends of her scarf. Becky waited, knowing a lecture was forthcoming. Whenever her father started up with his anti-skating, pro-fun routine, her mother felt constrained to defend him. It was part of their united parental front and very predictable.

"Don't be upset by what Daddy said," her mother began.

"Mom, I'm not upset, but wouldn't you think that by now he'd have given it up?"

"Not your father. He's not the type who gives up. He's too stubborn. Look, he only does it because he loves you and wants you to be happy. His father died when he was fourteen, and he was left the head of the family. By time he was your age, he was already an adult. He never *had* a childhood."

"But *I* can't do anything about that," Becky replied. "I can't relive his childhood for him. Anyway, his idea of happiness is one thing; mine's another. I wouldn't be happy being the girl he wants me to be, Ms. Typical American Teenager. I'm happy being *me*, a skater."

Her mother continued twisting the fringes around in her fingers — long, bony fingers with nails filed short, the kind of capable, no-nonsense fingers that looked as though they could do anything. She shot Becky a smile that was almost apologetic. "You don't have to convince *me*. I was a skater too once, remember? But your father's no athlete . . ."

"*That's* the understatement of the century!"

"That's why it's so hard for him to understand. Remember when you were working on the triple? He couldn't bear to come and watch. He was sure you'd kill yourself, or at the very least, break every bone in your body. He thought what you

18

were doing was physically impossible. But look, even though he worries and fights it, one thing you can be sure of. Despite all the fussing and nagging, when you're up there on that winners' platform with that gold medal around your neck, he'll be going around telling everyone in sight, 'That's my little girl. I always knew she was a winner!'"

"Yeah, but until then he'll keep on driving me crazy, hassling me," Becky sighed. She sat there staring out the car window. Cal, one of the custodians, was driving the big, yellow snowplow out of the shed to clear a path in the snow. A couple of little kids came running out after it, kicking the snow back in its path as fast as Cal could clear it. "Mom?" Becky said in a small voice. "What if I *don't* make it?"

Her mother reacted right on cue and started to give the standard response. But Becky didn't want to hear the standard response. Not this time. This time she wanted to talk about reality, not Disneyville, to confide her fear and have her mother accept it as legitimate and real. "Mom, please don't patronize me, okay? I'm not a baby anymore. We both know there's a possibility I might not qualify at the Nationals. It could happen. There's certainly enough competition. Good skaters. *Great* ones like Fratianne and Allen. You've seen them skate. You *know*. They could annihilate me. Or I could just get unlucky and skate badly, or there could be somebody else, a dark horse, like that girl at Hartford last year, the one from Buffalo with the heavy legs."

"You know what Vera says," her mother murmured, busily knotting and unknotting the fringes. "You've got to *believe* you're going to win; believe it not just in your head, but down in your gut where it counts. Confidence! It's even more important than talent, training, and skill. When you really believe you're a winner, you turn out to be one."

"Mom, that's fine for you to say, but I can't walk around all the time telling myself fairy tales. I'm not an idiot, you know, thinking positive twenty-four hours a day. You know when it hits me? In the middle of the night. I wake up, and I say to myself, *'What if I don't make it?'* Then I panic. I can't stop thinking. I lie there all night, worrying myself sick. I wish I could be like Dee. She wants to make it, sure, but she isn't going to lie down and die if she doesn't. Skating's important to her, but it's not her whole life the way it is mine."

Her mother tucked the scarf ends inside her jacket. She looked at Becky with a thoughtful expression. "Lovey, Dee wants to make it every bit as badly as you do. She's just more defensive, that's all. She doesn't want to go all out and make an upfront commitment on the chance she doesn't win. Then she wants to be able to walk away saying, 'It's okay. Because I didn't really want it all that much, anyway.' No, it's true, believe me. I've been where Dee is, and I know all the signs. Dee wants it just as much as you do. She's just not as open and honest about it."

Becky exclaimed, immediately on the defensive, "But she is! Dee's the most honest, open person I know." She shot her mother a look. They both knew it wasn't true, but she wouldn't have thought of being disloyal to her best friend. "Hey, don't mind me, okay? It's just my usual, pre-performance hysteria starting up right on schedule."

"I know. Don't worry about it."

Becky reached into the back seat for her things. "See you tonight, Mom. And thanks!" She waited for the Volvo to cough into action before climbing out. She was thinking about all the times her mother had been there for her, putting herself and her own needs second after Becky's. All the times she had been cheerfully packed up to trek off around the country to competitions, exhibitions, and meets, all the hours she spent laboring over Becky's costumes. With her talent she could have had a career as a designer, a decorator. She didn't have to sit home being chief cook, seamstress, chauffeur, and chaperone. Sometimes Becky couldn't help but wonder. What did her mother get out of it, other than secondhand glory? What was there in it all for *her*? She turned back, her hand on the door. "Know what, Mom? As mothers go, you rate about a ten-plus-plus!" she said, grinning.

Her mother shot her a smile. "Thanks! I kind of like you, too," she replied, and drove off.

CHAPTER FOUR

Becky pushed through the turnstile outside the ticket booth. Mrs. Williams smiled and waved. Mrs. Williams had been a pro once, in the Ice Capades, or so she was always saying. She was pretty old now, and crippled up with arthritis, so she couldn't skate anymore. She spent nine-tenths of her waking hours at the rink. It was the only place she wanted to be.

Mrs. Williams had been working as ticket-taker ever since Becky started coming to the rink. Rick, the rink manager, had told Becky that the Parks Department had hired her because they felt sorry for her, but Becky seriously doubted that the bureaucratic Parks Department was endowed with so much soul. Mrs. Williams had probably agreed to work cheap in exchange for the questionable privilege of being allowed to work a sixty-hour week for two-and-a-quarter an hour, plus benefits.

Becky entered the rink, shivering involuntarily as the damp cold hit her. *"That's what happens to skaters when they can't skate anymore,"* she thought. It was a young sport. The time to start was when you were real little. If you hadn't passed the first three tests by the time you were eight or nine, you were running behind. If you hadn't finished your silver and your gold by your mid-teens, you were a lost cause.

When you were a serious, dedicated skater, skating was your life, a better than full-time commitment that left you no time for anything else. You skated eight, ten hours a day, seven days a week, sometimes more. And, if you were a kid, it didn't just involve *you* either. She knew skaters whose families had rearranged their whole lives, picked up, moved across country, given up their homes, their jobs, their friends. Only a few of the best skaters made it, and even the best didn't make it sometimes. You knew the odds were stacked against you, but you kept on going, hoping you'd be one of the lucky ones and wind up another Dorothy Hamill or Peggy Fleming.

Becky pushed open the door of the pro shop. Rick came out of his office and made a beeline for her, super-jock in an electric-blue warmup suit that matched his eyes. When she had been younger, she had had a crush on Rick Arnetta, but that had been B.J., Before Jed.

"Hey, B.B., why are you limping? Something wrong with your leg?"

"I strained a muscle during my lesson yesterday."

"That's a bummer! But hang in there, B.B. A gymnast in the last summer Olympics competed in four events after breaking his leg in six places."

"Sure it wasn't six events and four places?"

Rick headed for his office, and she sat down on a bench to put on her skates. She could hardly bend over, she had so many layers of clothing on. She was one skater who refused to work out in an unheated rink half-naked. Someday, maybe, the Town Board would get around to voting enough money to heat the place. Until then she intended to skate looking like "The Abominable Snowperson." She wasn't going to freeze her rear end off for anybody, even Vera.

"All dat clothink interferz mit your skatink," Vera was constantly saying.

"So will double pneumonia," Becky would mutter under her breath.

A few of the younger kids were sitting around the fireplace yakking and drinking cocoa. One of them called over, "Becky, did you see the list for Sunday? Gosh, is there ever an exhibition you and Dee don't skate in?"

"Never," Becky replied. Wouldn't you think just once Vera would take pity on at least one of them and let them off the hook? But no. Not

"Vera The Relentless" — the orneriest, toughest, most demanding pro in the business. She had a Grade A fit if they even suggested not skating in one of her old exhibitions.

Becky slipped her bare feet into her skates, wincing as the calf muscle flexed, then knotted in rebellion. Her skates were practically brand-new, only six months old, but they looked ancient. They had been custom-made for her by Larry Zelkow, the master skatemaker — rock-hard leather uppers, glove-leather linings, specially built-up soles to withstand the constant friction of the edges against the ice, the wear and tear of her seemingly effortless, but actually very hard, skating. Already the edges were worn way down, and the hand-crafted, stainless-steel blades had had to be resharpened four times. She was unusually hard on her equipment, which meant her parents were constantly having to invest in replacements. It was a very guilt-making, especially when you considered that just blades ran well over a hundred dollars, and the cost of custom-made Zelkows had just gone up to four-hundred a pair. Add to that the fact that Vera charged more for lessons than any pro in the East, all the money for travel, private ice time, clothing, test fees, club membership, etc., and her skating was costing over twelve-thousand dollars a year. Luckily, since becoming a regional champion, she was being subsidized by her club, The Skating

Club of New York. Otherwise, she might have had to drop out of the running long ago. Even though he was doing pretty well in his own printing business, her father couldn't have gone on spending that kind of money indefinitely.

Dee's parents spent four times as much, and Dee wasn't being subsidized. She could have been, but her parents refused to accept any financial help. Of course, they could easily afford to finance *four* skaters, but still, it was a lot of money. Dee's costumes were all made by the designer who did the costumes for the ice shows. They cost a mint. She had a whole slew of them. She had a lot more than Becky, a lot more than any skater needed. Still her mother was constantly buying more, pushing for extra lessons, more private ice time, anything that would further Dee's skating career. It made Dee crazy, and it worried Becky. She knew Dee. Her tolerance level was dangerously low, especially when it came to her mother. One day, if Mrs. Danziger wasn't careful, Dee would stage a rebellion, take off her skates, and never put them on again.

Becky was just finishing lacing up her skates when Dee staggered in, a half hour late, gorgeous in a plum-pink, quilted down jumpsuit and a pink-and-orange ski cap and matching scarf. Her dark curls tumbled out from under the cap, framing her heart-shaped face with its perfect features and accentuating her huge green eyes. She collapsed on the bench with a groan. "Shh! Don't speak. Dee-Dee's still sleeping," she whispered, putting her head on Becky's shoulder.

Becky gave the head a pat. "Love your new jumpsuit. It's very chic. And the color's perfect. It matches your bloodshot eyes. Tell me, Cinderella, what time did you get home from the ball last night?"

"About one." Dee squinted up at her out of one eye.

"What did your parents say when you came waltzing in at that hour?"

"Nothing. They weren't home. They were in the city seeing a Broadway show. That's part of my father's latest save-our-marriage campaign. Not that it'll work. That marriage is just too far gone. It's incapable of being revived at this point."

"Oh, I don't know. Marriages are funny that way," Becky mused. "Take my aunt and uncle, for instance. They were divorced a whole year when they happened to run into one another in California, fell madly in love, and decided to get married again."

"Well, that's California, not New York." Dee took a pack of gum from her pocket, unwrapped three pieces and popped them into her mouth.

Flo Swensen and Tami Morse came in. Flo was wearing just a skating dress, a sweater, and tights. Just looking at her made Becky shiver.

"Flo, aren't you freezing?"

"I'm numb, but you won't catch me covering up these old legs of mine. I'm going to show them while I still have them to show. What's with Danziger? Did she die?"

"She's just catching up on her sleep."

Flo was in her forties, but she didn't look it. She had a terrific face and a great figure. She had been a pro once like Mrs. Williams, but, unlike Mrs. Williams, she had never stopped skating. She worked out at the rink every morning for at least one session, usually two and even three. She said it was to keep herself in shape, but Becky knew better. Flo didn't have anything else to do. She had no other interests, no career, no family. When she had been young, she had devoted herself completely to her skating. Now it was all she had.

"I'm giving Tami her first skating lesson," Flo said, bending down to help Tami off with her boots. Becky and Dee exchanged glances. Tami was around twelve, but she looked younger, mainly because she was so small. She had some kind of orthopedic problem and had to wear steel clamps on her hips and sometimes a neck brace. She was a skating bug and spent so much time hanging around the rink, she knew more about skating than the pros. Until now her parents had been afraid to let her try it. A few weeks ago Tami had come up with a brainstorm. She would get Flo, the ex-pro, to approach her parents and talk them into letting Flo give her some lessons. They'd know that with good old Flo in charge, she would be safe.

"Some gutsy kid," Dee murmured.

"I don't know whether she's gutsy, dumb, or just plain crazy," Becky replied. Everything was relative. Here she was thinking she'd lie down and die of a broken heart if she didn't qualify in the Nationals and skate in next year's Olympics, and Tami Morse was thrilled just to be able to put on a pair of skates and stand upright on the ice.

"Would you mind removing your head from my shoulder, Danziger Darling? The session's about to begin." Dee sat up, yawned widely, reached into her pocket, and extracted the gum. She began to unwrap the pieces and pop them into her mouth one by one. "Danziger, your dentist must love you. Bet you're his favorite patient."

"Mmmm, yrr, I guess," Dee mumbled, giving out with an enormous yawn. Like Becky's father, she was definitely *not* a morning person. "Where are you going?" she called as Becky limped toward the exit. "How can you leave me here like this? Some best friend you are, Rebecca Bacall!"

Much as she would have liked to have stayed and rapped, Becky couldn't spare the time. Not now with the exhibition four days away and a strained calf muscle to contend with. She slipped off her skate guards, put them on the barrier, and stepped out on to the ice, giving out with a yelp as the calf muscle went into another spasm.

"What's the matter, Becky?" Tami asked, coming out the exit door behind her.

"A little cramp, that's all," Becky gasped, bending to knead the muscle with her fingers.

"Yeah, I get those lots of times," Tami confided, watching her with big eyes. "Skating has its drawbacks too, doesn't it? But who cares about a little pain when you can do *that*?"

She watched with worshipful eyes as Becky pushed off and started stroking. Becky always stroked the rink six times at the start of every practice session to warm up, get her body moving and the oxygen flowing. After the stroking came the figures, and then the freeskating. Today she would spend some extra time on that. There were going to be three Olympic Committee judges watching her skate at Sky Rink on Sunday. She had to be perfect.

Sky Rink. A pretty prestigious place, come to think of it, and just about the best skating rink in the New York City area. It was also the rink where her skating club was based. A lot of top skaters skated there. On any given day you could usually see two or three, plus a lot of other famous and semifamous people. But it wasn't because Sky was chic, or frequented by famous people, that she preferred it to any rink but Northridge. It was because the ice was always so well-groomed, so smooth, slick, and glossy, and because it was heated. And that meant that even on the coldest days you could work out in just tights, a sweater, and leg warmers.

She began her figures, starting with the loops, doing them over and over again, one on top of the other, until there was a giant tracing etched into the ice. She was deep into concentration now, totally immersed in what she was doing. There were other people on the ice, but she wasn't aware of them. The pain in her leg had been forgotten. She had put it aside. The only things she was conscious of were the feel of her blades cutting the ice, the rhythm of her body responding to internal commands, the knowledge that, no matter how hard she worked, or how expert at this she became, there was always the possibility that there was someone out there even better whom she would ultimately have to compete with.

CHAPTER FIVE

She was working on the newest addition to her repertoire, the jump-spin she was going to perform for the first time in public at Sky on Sunday, when Dee came tearing over, her dark curls blowing out behind her, a big grin on her face.

"That was incredible! Absolutely perfect. Not even one fraction of a centimeter off from start to finish. Hamill couldn't have done it better, Beck. I mean it."

"Well, let's not get carried away," Becky laughed, feeling pleased. She put her hands on her hips and pressed downward, stretching her spine to get the kinks out. "I'm a wreck," she sighed, shifting her tailbone, hearing several of her less stable vertebrae crack. "I could hardly get out of bed this morning." She checked out the clock, gave her spine one last stretch and said, "Look at the time. We'd better get to work."

"Groan, yawn, and other various and sundry evidences of boredom. Don't you ever get tired of being so madly industrious all the time?"

Becky bent to retie her skate laces, looking up at Dee from behind the mop of hair that had fallen into her eyes. "I'm not this industrious *all* the time," she said in a defensive tone, "but, if I was ever going to be madly industrious, it would certainly be now, two months before the National Championships."

Dee shrugged, looking aggravated. "Okay, stop. I get the message. But I can't live just for skating. I've got to have something else in my life. It makes me crazy if I don't. I get uptight and do weird things and freak out. Maybe, if I had a boyfriend like Jed, I wouldn't mind it so much, though sometimes I wonder. Doesn't he ever get tired of playing second fiddle to a pair of figure skates?"

"If he does, he hasn't mentioned it," Becky replied complacently. Dee started to skate away. Becky put a hand on her arm. "Dee, it's only two months. You can hack it for two months, can't you? It'll all be worth it when we're up there, the Dynamic Duo, the best on blades, together in the Olympics!"

Dee started to reply. Just then Rick called over the loudspeaker, "Hey, B.B., how about a sneak preview of that piece you're skating at Sky on Sunday?"

"Boy, Arnetta, are you rude!" Dee shouted across to him. "You interrupted us right in the middle of a conversation."

"Danziger, you're *always* in the middle of a conversation. How about it, B.B.? For the Prez of your fan club?"

"And the V.P.," Flo called over.

"And your favorite groupie," Tami chimed in.

Becky smiled, feeling good. It sure was nice being surrounded by people who were so positive about you all the time, a lot more positive, in fact, that you often were about yourself. She glanced at the clock. It was still early. And she had been planning on running through the piece anyway. It was something she had choreographed herself to music from *Giselle*, her favorite ballet. Vera had wanted her to use *Swan Lake. Swan Lake?* Every skater since Sonya Henie had skated to *that*!

"Do *Swan Lake* and the judges'll be too busy throwing up to notice you," Dee had said. "What are you, a woman or a mouse? Tell the old crow you won't do it!"

Rick put her music on. Becky took her position, head high, chin up, shoulders back. She pushed off, glided forward, and gained momentum with a series of lightning-fast turning maneuvers around the rink. She lifted off into the axel, clearing the ice as though she were weightless. There was a burst of applause from the group gathered at the barrier, but Becky didn't hear it. She was too engrossed in her performance. She went into the spread eagle, leaning so far out over her edges, her boots scraped the ice; moved into the triple-toe loop, the leg lift, a flying sit-spin that turned her body into a blur of motion; came out of it in an attitude finish, down on one knee, the other leg extended in front of her, head thrown back, both arms above her head in a ballerina's pose. The music swelled, then faded. She held the position an instant longer. No one seeing the look on her face at that moment would have doubted that Becky Bacall was doing the one thing in the world she had been born to do and doing it to perfection.

"We better hurry. It's getting late," she said when she and Dee were in the locker room getting dressed.

"Plenty of time," Dee mumbled, bending over to buckle the straps of the spike-heeled sandals that transformed her five-foot-three inches into five-foot-seven. She wiggled into her jeans, jumped up and down to get them up over her hips, sucked in her gut, and zipped them. The minute she let out her breath, they came unzipped again. "I love spike heels with tight jeans, don't you?" she gasped, sucking in again and rezipping.

"Tight? Those jeans aren't just tight. They're like skin. If they were any tighter, *you* wouldn't be wearing *them*. *They'd* be wearing *you*!"

"Do you adore these shoes? They're *chere Maman's*, but she let me borrow them. Remember how manic she used to get when I asked to borrow any of her things? Now she can't wait to lend them to me. It's all part of the bribe to get me to skate in the Olympics." She stuck out one foot and surveyed it with a smug expression. "Aren't they *divine*? Know what they cost? Sixty-nine-ninety-nine. On sale at Bloomie's."

Becky was aghast. "Sixty-nine-ninety-nine for three skinny straps and one precariously high heel? What a ripoff! Bet my mother never paid more than thirty dollars for a pair of shoes in her life."

"Sure she did. She just lied about the price to your father, just like mine does," Dee giggled. She wound her belt twice around her waist, buckled it over the baggy purple sweater with the big, floppy sleeves, got her makeup case out of her bookbag and began doing things to her face.

"Why do you use all that gunk?" Becky asked. "Don't you know you're gorgeous without it?"

"You really think so?" Dee stepped back, watching herself in the mirror. She began to dance around the dressing room, singing at the top of her lungs, *"I feel pretty. I feel pretty. I feel pretty and witty and wiiisse. It's a pity. That I haven't got a date to-niiiight!"*

Becky burst out laughing. She gathered up her things. Still dancing, Dee twirled out the door. Becky followed her, thinking, if she was only going to get one real, true friend in her life, she sure was glad it was Dee!

CHAPTER SIX

The day was cold and incredibly clear. There was all that sparkling-clean fresh snow on the ground from last night's snowstorm, and it crunched under their feet as they trudged up Vista Hill. In the distance the clock tower of Northridge High gleamed against a brilliant blue sky.

"I love this kind of day, don't you?" Becky said, filling her lungs with air. "The air's so brisk, so invigorating!"

Dee shot her a sour look. "Some meteorologist on the news this morning said the air quality would be unacceptable today."

"Oh, really? Well, then I won't breathe 'til tomorrow."

A horn honked, and a little red Triumph

pulled over. Danny Pharaoh stuck his head out the window and called, "Hey, girls. Want a lift?"

"My hero!" Dee scrambled into the front seat, snuggling up beside Danny, which left Becky to maneuver her five-feet-seven-inches into the back. She sat there with her knees up underneath her chin, feeling idiotic.

"Nice car, Danny. Is it new?" Danny didn't reply. He hadn't even heard her. He was intent on ogling Dee, who was intent on ogling him back. Becky felt a lot like the Invisible Woman. "Yes, it's new, Becky," she muttered, glowering at the back of Danny's head. "Glad you like it."

"Are you going to Chrissy's party Saturday night?" Danny asked Dee.

Dee dimpled up, batted her baby greens, and said, "Sure! Are you?" Becky went into shock. Was Dee playing games, or was she really contemplating going to a party Saturday night when the exhibition was Sunday morning?

Becky had gotten an invitation to the party too, but she hadn't even given a thought to going — not the night before a performance. Not *any* performance, but especially not this one.

"Will I see you tonight?" Danny said to Dee when they pulled into the school parking lot.

She gave him a flirtatious look and said in a sexy voice, "Maybe."

"What d'you mean, *maybe*? Gimme a yes or a no!"

Dee shot him an ego-shriveling glance, climbed

out of the car, and flounced away. Danny sat there looking nonplussed, staring after her.

"Well, thanks for the lift, Danny," Becky said, extricating herself. "It sure is a nice car!" She took off after Dee, catching up with her at the bottom of the steps. "Hey, why'd you give him a rough time? I thought you were madly in love with him."

"I *am* madly in love with him, silly. That's *why*! See, Danny's the type of boy who once he knows a girl's hooked on him loses interest right away. So, if I want to keep him, I have to keep him guessing; get what I mean?"

Becky burst out laughing. "Dee Danziger, I don't believe you said that. You, who're so pro-feminist and all, so women's lib. If the feminists heard you, they'd take away your membership card and drum you out of the corps." She followed Dee up the stairs thinking her friend sure was a mass of inconsistencies. One minute she was one person, the next, someone else. You never knew what to expect, but then, that was part of her charm, her spontaneity and unpredictability.

"You have to play the game if you want to be popular," Dee was saying. "You would too if it were you and Jed."

Becky shot her a surprised look. "But I wouldn't have to," she exclaimed, limping after her through the double doors. "Jed and I were friends first, remember, long before there was

41

ever anything romantic happening between us. We always had the same honest, fifty-fifty kind of friendship you and I have."

"Sure, sure, sure," mumbled Dee, turning away.

A bunch of girls were gathered in the hallway outside the main office. "You didn't mean it, did you, when you said you were going to Chrissy Raines's party?" Becky asked, smiling and waving to them.

Sue Farber came out of the math lab, her nose buried in a book.

"Wake up, Sue," Dee said, sidestepping to avoid a collision.

Sue looked up, blinked at them from behind her bifocals, then broke into a smile, her braces glinting in the gleam from the overhead lights. "Oh, hi!" was all she said. If the subject didn't have something to do with math or science, Sue was at a loss.

"I like your dress," Becky offered.

"*Do* you? I don't know why I bought it. It's not my style of dress at all."

"Did you ever see anything so *huge*?" Dee whispered when Sue walked away. "She looks like an ostrich in that dress. Why'd you say you liked it?"

"Because I *do*!" Becky felt guilty. It was catty of Dee to say that. Becky would have died if anyone had said a thing like that about her, but Dee was right. Sue did look like an ostrich, in the dress or out of it.

The bell rang, and she hurried off. She didn't want to be late again and earn another demerit to add to her collection. It wasn't easy to limp and hurry at the same time, but she managed. It seemed her whole life she was either racing to or from something, always on the verge of being late. In her family punctuality was a phobia. Her father had a real thing about that, and she had inherited it from him.

Dee's homeroom was all the way on the other side of the school. They didn't have any classes together, so they wouldn't be seeing each other until lunchtime. Lunchtime, what a joke! For Becky that was a fast, frantic fifteen minutes between fourth and fifth periods when she bolted down whatever was quick and handy.

She charged into homeroom and fell into her seat just as the final bell was ringing.

"Yes, ladies and gentlemen. Once again Limping Lena saves the day, just in the nick of time!"

Ms. Parker. Having her for a homeroom teacher was a fate worse than death. When you were late, she practically had you stretched on the rack. She wished she could dispense with homeroom, a real time-waster, and go straight to her first-period class, her favorite class of all time, psychology. Ms. Wing, her psych instructor, was her idea of a really gifted teacher, really sharp and hip and with it — what a teacher ought to be like. You never got bored in Ms. Wing's class, not even if you were the type who hated school and every class in it. Ms. Wing never gave lectures. She never talked *at* you; she talked *with* you. The class sat around for an hour twice a week rapping, talking about things that interested them, sharing their feelings and their views. Once in a while Ms. Wing would throw out an idea, a theory, or a hypothesis. Then the class would get into it, discuss it, kick it around. You never realized you had learned anything until later, when a light bulb went on inside your head all of a sudden, and you said to yourself, *"My gosh! I think I just learned something."*

"You have an intuitive understanding of people and what makes them tick," Ms. Wing had written on Becky's evaluation form that every teacher had to write at the end of the first marking period. "Perhaps you'll want to consider a career in some psychologically oriented field: psychiatry, counseling, or psychiatric social work. If you'd like to discuss it, I'm available."

Becky hadn't liked to discuss it, particularly with Ms. Wing, the last person in the world she would want to find out that after graduation she wasn't going on to college as originally planned. Sure, it had always been taken for granted she would. Her parents had been saving for years. Her decision, made just a few months ago, had shaken them, and they were still reeling from the shock and disappointment. They didn't understand why she was doing this and no matter how she tried to explain they probably never would. Mainly she just felt she couldn't go on under this much pressure anymore. Things were bad enough right now, and this was high school. Imagine what it would be like trying to cope with *college* and still keep up with the skating. She was sixteen, pretty old for a skater. It was now or never. If she didn't make next year's Olympics, she'd never get another chance. She couldn't handle two such time-consuming and demanding things as college *and* skating and do justice to either. If one was going to go, it had to be college, because skating, well, she'd die before she'd give *that* up.

"Hey, Becky," Sean Mercer called to her in his *macho* voice. "Do you need a lift to the party Saturday night? I got a new car. I'll pick you up."

"You got it?" one of the boys called over. "The Mustang you were talking about?"

"No, it's a Pinto," Sean replied, trying to sound thrilled. He was about to go on, but Ms. Parker, the homeroom teacher, came back in, and everyone snapped to attention. She swept the room with her gaze, as if to say, *"Yes, I know you're all terrified of me, and that's just the way I like it!"* She was the toughest teacher of all time. Everyone was afraid of her, even the principal, Mr. Tucker.

Just then a kid came in with a note from the main office. Ms. Parker read it and followed him out of the room. Chrissy Raines leaned across the aisle and whispered, "I'm sorry you can't come to my party."

"Me too, Chrissy. There's this really important exhibition in the city Sunday morning, and I'm skating in it. I have to get to bed real early Saturday night."

"You're not coming to the orgy of the century?" Sean drawled, leering at her across the aisle.

"No, I'm not."

"Gee, I wouldn't want to be a skater," Chrissy mused. "You have to give up a lot when you're a skater." Becky nodded, shifting uneasily in her seat. The way Sean was looking at her made her feel like something under a microscope in Mrs. Finkel's science class.

"Hey, it's too bad you can't make it," Sean said when he caught up with her in the hall after homeroom. "If I know the Raineses, it'll be a blast."

"Yeah, well, that's the way it goes," she muttered. Well, one good thing anyway. If she didn't go to Chrissy's party, she didn't have to spend Saturday evening being pored over by Sean Mercer's pop eyes.

CHAPTER
SEVEN

"Psych was unreal," Becky said to Dee when they were on their way back to the rink after school. "We did this experiment. Everybody switched roles. The boys were girls, and the girls, boys. It was fascinating to see how everybody reacted. If I weren't a skater, I think I'd be a psychiatrist, or a social worker, or something like that."

"Who says you can't be both?" Dee queried, pulling her coat collar up and her ski cap down over her eyes. "A skater *and* a psychiatrist. A person can be more than one thing, you know. It's not against the law. Take me, for instance. I'm a skater too, right? I'm also a scuba diver, dancer, artist, and a whole bunch of other fascinating things. I've got a lot of talents I want to develop, I've decided. If the Fashion Institute of

Technology accepts me, I'm going in the fall. I'm going to be the biggest fashion designer in the East. I don't want to stick just with skating and wind up someday like Flo Swensen, or Mrs. Williams, or Vera. I want more out of life than ugly feet, arthritis, and a lifelong case of the chills!"

"But that's different," Becky protested, slowing her pace so Dee could catch up. "You're an artist. Art's a special gift. One you're born with. I don't have any special gifts, other than skating."

"Psyching people out. That's *your* special gift," Dee replied with a shrug. "You just said it yourself, that if you weren't a skater, you'd be a psychiatrist. So? Look at it this way. Say you make the Olympics, win the gold medal. So then what? You go pro, spend the next few years skating a show, John Curry's or Toller Cranston's, the Ice Capades maybe. You hit twenty-nine, thirty, get a few wrinkles, veins in your legs. Let's face it, nobody hires a skater with wrinkles and veiny legs. So now where are you? Going downhill fast. You never took the time to get a college education, so you haven't any skills besides skating. If you've found time to fit it in, maybe you've gotten married, had a few kids. *Maybe*, but more likely you've just devoted your whole life to skating, the way you are now."

"For a generally cheerful person, you sure can be depressing!" Becky grumbled, zipping her parka up to her chin. She wished Dee would leave it be. She wasn't in the mood for a hassle. Anyway, it was enough she had her parents on her case. She didn't need her best friend, too.

"Look, I'm not like you," she began. "A natural talent . . ." She stopped, feeling flustered. Dee was giving her this look, as though she had said something totally out of line. But why? What Becky had said was true. Dee *was* a natural. She'd never had to work anywhere near as hard at it as Becky. She was so much more the physical type, too. She had "star quality," that special something that made her unique, set her apart from other skaters. And she had style, the kind of style that made audiences sit up and take notice, then fall in love with her.

Okay, so maybe she didn't drive herself as hard as Becky did. Maybe she didn't put skating before everything else in her life either. But then, she didn't have to. She was a natural-born skater so she could make it without doing those things.

Dee turned around and flounced away. She wasn't wearing flouncing shoes, though, and anyway it was difficult to flounce in ten inches of snow. Suddenly she slipped on a patch of ice and would have fallen if Becky hadn't caught her just in time.

"Damn!" Dee growled, giving the patch of ice a savage kick. "I hate this weather. I hate ice. I hate snow. I hate being cold! One of these days I'm going to take off and go somewhere where it's always warm and sunny, where it never rains, and it never snows, where I'll never have to be cold again!"

"Let me know when you're leaving. I'll come and see you off." Becky attempted to help her perambulate the snowdrift alongside the sidewalk, but Dee shrugged her hand away. It wasn't until they were practically at the rink that she recovered her amiability.

"I've got the greatest idea!" she cried excitedly. "How we can go to Chrissy's party and not take a chance on messing up Sunday morning."

"Oh, no. Not again!"

"No, listen. It's called making a compromise, a thing lots of people do when they're faced with a problem."

"I'm not facing a problem, Dee. I've already made my decision. And besides, skaters who make compromises don't get to skate in the Olympics."

"Oh!" Dee growled, giving her arm a pinch. "You make me so mad sometimes, I could just *kill* you!" She bent down, scooped up a handful of snow, strolled over, and stuffed it down Becky's collar. Becky screeched as it slid slowly down her back.

"You little fink!" she cried, grabbing some snow and dumping it down Dee's sweater before she could get away. Dee picked up another handful and aimed it at Becky's face. Becky backed away, slipped and fell. Dee jumped on her. In a moment they were rolling around, finding new and original places to put the snow. Dee got some down Becky's jeans. Becky put a fistful in Dee's ear. It wound up a free-for-all. It had been ages since they'd done anything like this, crazy and wild, just for fun, a chance to let off steam. It felt good to laugh and scream and be silly for a change.

"We ought to do this more often," Becky said, brushing snow out of her hair. "It's fun!"

Dee gave her a look. "Well, well! It's nice to know you still remember how to *have* fun, Super Skater."

"Come, come," Vera said, shooing her out on the ice. "Vee get to vork!" She lumbered along behind Becky looking like a grizzly bear in a big mouton coat out of a 1940's movie. "Rebecca, are you limpink? The legg, it shtill hurts?"

"Oh, no. It's fine, Vera."

"Goot! Dat is becausze you follow Vera's instructionsz, yes?"

"Yes!"

"So, if it iss all better, how come you shtill limp?"

"Am I limping? Really? Force of habit, I guess."

"So! Vee do dee figuresz, startink mit dee eightsz. Back shraight, chinz up, shouldersz back, und *schmile*!"

"*Achtung!*" Becky thought, forcing a half-hearted simper.

51

Vera watched with appraising eyes. "You are sure the legg iss all better?"

"Well, maybe it still hurts a little . . ."

"Aha! So. Vee must vork an extra haff hour today. The vay you are movink, you need it."

Oh, no! Just what she needed to put her even further behind schedule. She began the loops, telling herself not to panic, but she couldn't stop thinking about how that extra half hour was going to get her to bed late again, as usual. She knew it was no use arguing. You didn't argue with the whole Russian military rolled up in one large, dominating, stubborn woman dressed up as a cossack from the War of 1812. If Vera told you you had to do something, you did it or else; or else Vera would dump you, thereby ending your dreams of ever skating *anywhere*, much less in the Olympics. As Vera was always telling her students, she didn't *have* to teach. She only did it out of pure, unadulterated good-naturedness, and, if you did anything to deflate that good-naturedness, she would cross you off her list.

"Rebecca, vouldt you mindt tellink me vat iss dat you are doink?"

"A loop, Vera."

"A loop? *Phah!* It looksz more like a brackedt to me."

"I'm sorry." Becky started over again, focusing on doing it right, willing herself to concentrate. She mustn't let herself start daydreaming.

Daydreaming. That was an offense punishable by death and very uncharacteristic of her.

"Rebecca, how am I supposed to know if you are doink it right ven you are vearink so much clothink? Vye do you insiszt on vearing so much clothink? Vere do you think you are, the North Pole?"

"*Siberia,*" Becky thought, staring glumly at her skate boots. She tried to focus on what Vera was saying, but sneaky little thoughts kept worming their way into her brain.

"Rebecca, you are not listenink!" Vera bellowed at her.

"I'm listening, Vera. I am. Really." Not listening, that was another criminal offense, as despicable and foul as child beating.

Vera was looking at her oddly. "Are you feelink all right? You don't look so goot. You haff gott big rinks under your eyesz. Are you gettink enough shleep or stayink up all night mit der friends?"

"*What friends?*" Becky thought glumly. "*I only have one.*" She got back to work. She could feel Vera's eyes boring into her. Sometimes, when Vera looked at you with those little, piggy eyes, you got so nervous you couldn't do *anything* right.

"Maybe vee skip itt, der extra haff hour," Vera said, almost smiling. "The vay you are lookink today, an extra haff hour of shleep vould make more sensze."

Becky was so shocked, so overwhelmed with gratitude, she forgot to stay cool. "Oh, Vera, thank you!" Vera gave her a look, and she blushed and dropped her eyes. You just didn't get familiar with Vera Berenkov. It wasn't done. Human contact, personal relationships, emotions, things like that didn't exist in Vera's world. She didn't approve of feelings, in her students or anyone else. Vera The Iceberg, that was her.

CHAPTER EIGHT

"I don't believe she was going to make you skate that extra half hour," Dee said when they were leaving the rink. "Honestly, that woman's *evil!*"

"Not evil. Just determined," Becky sighed, following her through the turnstile. "Gosh, I'm tired. I can't wait to get home. Do you want a lift?"

Dee shot her a guilty look. "Danny's picking me up. We're going to Friendly's. I'm not staying out, I promise, so don't look at me like that! I'll call you the minute I walk in the door and check in."

Becky laughed. The idea of Dee checking in with anybody was ludicrous. "Okay, but don't call during dinner. My parents have fits when anyone calls during dinner. Dinner at our house is sacrosanct."

"Well, don't knock it. Last time we sat down for a family dinner together was Thanksgiving, 1973, and that turned into a major marital crisis." She yanked her cap down over her ears, pulled up her collar, and began pacing back and forth in the snow, muttering disgruntedly about the weather. Danny arrived, and she took off with him, calling out the window, "Don't worry, Mommy. I going to be a good, wittle girl!" Becky watched the Triumph's taillights disappear, feeling kind of dejected and sad.

It wasn't because she had skated lousy. That could happen sometimes, even to the best skaters. You had a bad day, that's all, and blew a practice session, and, as long as it was only a practice session, it was okay. No, it wasn't the skating. It was a combination of other things, little things that when you added them all up together made one big thing. The party, for starters. Not that missing a party was anything unusual. She did it all the time on a regular basis. But this was kind of a special party, the last big party of the year, and her *senior* year, too. With Jed away at college her life was so dull. The weekends were just like weekdays, boring. It would have been nice to have had something special to do, something to look forward to and get dressed up for, something with people for a change instead of alone.

Life sure got dull when you never had anything special to do. Dee was right about that. She shivered, feeling the cold all the way down in her bones. Her stomach was feeling weird, but she guessed that was because she was hungry. She hadn't had time for anything all afternoon, and lunch had been ridiculous, a yogurt and an apple. She wished her mother would come. She was desperate to get home.

The Volvo came inching down the hill. Very uncharacteristic for her mother to inch. Inching, that was more her father's style. The Volvo pulled up alongside, and Becky opened the door.

"Beanie, you look like Rudolph the Red-Nosed Reindeer," her father laughed. "Why didn't you wait inside?"

"Daddy, hi! What're *you* doing here?"

"Your mother's making eggplant parmigiana. She's up to her eyeballs in tomato sauce and mozzarella cheese, so I said I'd come to pick you up."

Becky climbed in beside him, grateful that Vera had decided to dispense with that extra half hour. "I think it's going to snow again. I can feel it in my bones," she said, reaching into the back for the car blanket. "Did you get the job, or are we going to go on living on principles indefinitely?"

"I got it," he said, pulling out of the parking lot. "And for fifteen-hundred dollars more than they originally offered. I'm getting to be some ruthless negotiator in my old age. Do you think it's the beard that intimidated them?"

He went on talking about his trip to Boston, telling her all these amusing anecdotes about how he had impressed the Board of Directors of A.M.I. so much they had awarded him the job, even though his bid was higher than anyone else's. Then all of a sudden he stopped, right in the middle of a sentence, and said, "Beanie, I phoned B.U. while I was there. They still want you."

She was amazed. Where had *that* come from, anyway? Boy, did he have lousy timing, starting his pro-college hassle at a time like this, moving in on her when he could see she was exhausted, and her defenses were down.

"Beanie," he went on in a pleading voice, "I'm not saying you shouldn't skate, just that you shouldn't make skating your *whole* life. How can you limit yourself that way? With an education you can be anything you want to be. Without it, you're just a skater."

She tried to keep her voice even, enunciating each syllable so he'd be sure to understand. *"That's exactly what I want to be, Daddy. A skater."*

"Beanie, please listen to me . . ."

"Daddy, is that why you offered to come and get me? So you could give me that lecture again, the one about my brilliant but wasted future? I just wish you'd have enough faith in me to realize I'm not a total idiot, that I know myself better than anybody and know what I'm doing. I can't hack it, the skating and college both, and I'm not going to make myself sick trying."

She suddenly realized she was shouting. Her tone had increased in volume in direct proportion to her emotions. She glanced over at him. His eyes were on the road, and he was pretending to be calm, but she could tell he was upset, and it made her feel guilty. He was just so sensitive and easily hurt, and once he got hurt he stayed that way for ages and ages. Not like her mother who got angry, had a screaming fit, got it all out of her system, then kissed and made up and a few minutes later had already forgotten what had made her angry in the first place.

"I'm sorry, Daddy," she murmured, watching his face. "I didn't mean to yell at you. Do you forgive me?"

He took his eyes off the road long enough to smile at her. "Of course I forgive you! I'm sorry too, Beanie. I won't nag you anymore, I promise."

"Okay, Daddy." Of course she knew that even though he promised, tomorrow, or the next day, or the next, he'd start the whole thing over again. That was his style.

They drove the rest of the way home in silence. They pulled into the driveway, and he turned off the ignition. The Volvo, unaware that it was now supposed to turn off, kept on going, reverberating under them like a steam engine.

"Well," she said, throwing open the door, "now that you're making all that money, you can afford to buy that Audi you've been drooling over at Bremmer Imports."

He smiled. The smile never quite made it from his lips up to his eyes. "I was thinking more along the lines of a Chevy or a Pontiac," he said, removing the keys from the ignition and dropping them into his pocket. "I've had it with foreign cars. Besides, the Audi's eleven thousand compared with seven or so for a Chevy or a Pontiac. Three or four thousand will pay for a lot of skating lessons, Beanie."

When they sat down to dinner, Becky realized she wasn't hungry. Her father watched her push a piece of eggplant around on her plate.

"I don't have much appetite," she explained, forcing down another mouthful to please him. Suddenly she was sick to her stomach, shivery and achey all over. She pushed her plate away, hoping that if they saw the shape she was in they'd take pity on her and let her out of the cleaning up.

"Okay, we get the message," her mother said, giving her a look. "Go on. Your father and I will clean up."

"Mom, you're the best!" Becky cried, jumping up from the table. She escaped upstairs, overwhelmed with gratitude. On her way up she heard her father say, "Sara, you're not being consistent," and her mother reply, "Alex, there are times in my life when consistent is the *last* thing on earth I want to be!"

"Good evening, Ronald Bear," Becky said, dropping her things on the floor, smiling at the frayed old Teddy bear on her bed. "Did you have a nice day?" She got out her assignment book and sat down at her desk, anxious to get her homework over and done with so she could get to bed. She would tackle the math first because it was the hardest. Luckily the assignment wasn't one she needed help with. Otherwise, she would have had to wait for the mathematical whiz kid, her mother, to finish and come upstairs.

"I *should* start that English paper," she muttered to herself, yawning for the twelfth time in a row. But an English paper, especially one assigned by Parker on a book as complex as Paul Zindel's *The Pigman*, wasn't something you did half-asleep. To do that kind of paper you had to be a hundred percent with it, wide awake, functioning at peak capacity. No, she would have to leave the paper until the weekend. As usual, while everyone else was at a party having a ball, she would be chained to her desk, plodding through a boring old English paper.

She got out her health text and scanned the assigned pages, but nothing was registering anymore. She was too far gone, too tired to concentrate. Her eyes kept going out of focus. Her head was beginning to ache, and her stomach was getting rambunctious. All she wanted was a lovely, long bath, a cup of hot cocoa, and bed, glorious bed!

Come to think of it, skip the cocoa. She was so beat, she would settle for just the bath and bed.

She headed down the hallway, peeling off her clothes along the way. She started to doze off in the tub. Groggily she climbed out, put on her pajamas, and groped her way back to her room.

"Sleep, glorious sleep!" she groaned, making a beeline for the bed. "Alarm clock, please don't feel rejected. I know you're there, and I'll set you later, I promise, but now *I just have to sleep*!"

She fell face down on the bed, so tired she didn't even have the energy to get under the covers. She opened one eye, checked out the clock, closed it again. "Eight-oh-one," she sighed. She was asleep before eight-oh-two.

CHAPTER NINE

She awoke with a headache and a funny pain in her stomach. She opened her eyes. There was sunlight streaming in through her windows. How could that be? Sunlight didn't stream through windows at a quarter to five in the morning.

She checked out the clock. *Nine-thirty?* She had overslept. But that was physically impossible. She was incapable of oversleeping. Didn't she have her handy, dandy, built-in electronic timer inside her head, keeping her always on schedule?

Her mother came in and said, "Well? All slept out?"

"Mom, why didn't you wake me?"

"Because you needed the sleep. I saw you'd forgotten to set your alarm, so I figured you must need sleep more than the practice session." She put the back of her hand against Becky's forehead, frowned, and said, "Are you sick?"

"I think I must be coming down with something. I have the world's *worst* headache, and my stomach's on the blink."

"Well, it's about time for you to come down with something. You haven't been sick since that virus last fall, remember? Stay in bed. No, no arguments. Mama is still the boss."

"Okay, Mama. You're still the boss," Becky giggled, thrilled to be taken charge of. The thought of having to get up made her feel giddy and weak all over.

"I'm going to call Doctor Arlen," her mother said, heading for the door. "Then I'm going to make you a nice, hot cup of tea with honey. Think you could eat a little something, or should we just stick with the tea for the time being?"

Doctor Arlen showed up a half hour later, looking like Errol Flynn in a pirate movie on the Late Show. Whenever he made a house call during the daytime, it was usually straight from the tennis court, the golf course, the stables where he kept his horse, the ski slopes, or some other really athletic-type place. Last time he'd been wearing this whole fancy riding outfit: jodhpurs, a hacking jacket, knee-high riding boots, a cravat, the hat, the whole equestrian ensemble.

"You look very spiffy," she said, smiling at him.

"Sorry I can't say the same for you." He

plunked his medical bag down on the bed, gave her a pinch on the cheek that all but paralyzed her from the neck up, took out his flashlight-looking gizmo, and spent the next five minutes getting intimately acquainted with her eyes, ears, nose, and throat. "Say 'ahhhh,' " he commanded, sticking a tongue depressor in her mouth, making her gag. He took out his stethoscope, pulled up her pajama top, and started tuning in to her chest. "Now breathe!"

Noisily she breathed in and out. "Gasp! Why are you examining my eyes, ears, nose, and throat, and listening to my chest, if the problem's in my stomach?"

He thumped her chest, and she coughed. "One of the symptoms may be discomfort in your stomach. The cause may originate somewhere else. Anyway, I have to examine all of you if I want to find out what's wrong. You want me to examine your stomach? Okay, I'll examine your stomach!"

"Ouch!" she yelped when he prodded her in the stomach with his finger. "Is that how you find out what's wrong with me? By jabbing me in the gut?"

He smiled benignly. "No, that's how I work out my hostilities. Now be quiet, and stop making like a comedian. You're making me nervous."

"*I'm* making *him* nervous!" Becky grumbled under her breath.

Finally he finished poking and prodding,

turned to her mother, and said, "Well, Sara, I can't find anything, except for some tenderness around the stomach. She seems healthy as a horse to me."

"Then why am I lying here like a wet noodle, Doctor Arlen?" Becky said, feeling threatened. "Because I'm healthy as a horse?"

"Marshall, Becky's not the type who imagines illnesses," her mother said.

"I'm not saying it's imaginary, Sara. Just that, at the moment, without doing a complete examination, I can't find anything, which doesn't mean there isn't something. She could very well be working on something: a virus, the flu" — he grinned at Becky — "Bubonic Plague. There are enough germs going around, and she's always rundown and susceptible. Let's keep her in bed a day or two and see what develops."

Becky shot him a bilious look. "And if it turns out to be Bubonic Plague, I'll take two aspirin and call you in the morning, right? Doctor Arlen, after taking care of me for sixteen years, you ought to know me well enough to know I don't make a habit of breaking out in psychosomatic symptoms, especially two days before an exhibition."

He smiled, turned to her mother and whispered, "Where did she learn *that*?"

"In her psychology class at school. Marshall, it's not easy living with a sixteen-year-old Sigmund Freud!"

The phone rang, and her mother hurried away to answer it. "Is there something bothering you, Becky?" Doctor Arlen asked when she was gone. "Something on your mind you'd like to talk about? Sometimes my patients prefer to talk to *me* rather than their parents, if you can believe such a thing. I have a feeling it's because I'm so understanding, compassionate, and sensitive."

"I'm not pregnant, if that's what you mean," Becky mumbled.

"*Pregnant?* When would you have time to get pregnant? You're too busy skating to get pregnant. There are a few other things a sixteen-year-old girl could have on her mind: a boyfriend, school, friends, the pressures of something as challenging as working toward skating in the Olympics." He sent her an Errol Flynn-buccaneer smile. "And from what I hear, you're going to be skating in the Olympics next year, so how about a couple of complimentary passes for your favorite family doctor?"

"Sure, favorite family doctor. Why not? Complimentary passes, plus an autographed eight-by-ten glossy of yours truly to hang on the wall in your office so everyone'll know you're the physician of a bona fide celebrity."

"He's a charmer, isn't he?" her mother said when she came back from showing Doctor Arlen out. "And a first-rate doctor, too."

"So, if he's so first rate, how come he couldn't

figure out what's wrong with me? He thought I was faking. Oh, yes he did! The minute you left the room, he started making like Marshall the Psychiatrist, asking me if I had problems, if there was something on my mind, the whole bit. Mom, *you* don't think I'm faking, do you?"

"You? Lovey, the thought never entered my mind!" Her mother came and sat down on the edge of the bed, looking at Becky the way she always did when she was about to become very maternal. "Look, *is* something bothering you? Because, if there is, you don't need to go to Marshall Arlen to talk about it. You've got me, and we've never had any difficulty bridging the generation gap. You know, you've really been pushing awfully hard lately. Sometimes, when we get strained and pressured and overtired, little problems suddenly seem big. Things get out of proportion. Things you can usually handle with no difficulty at all seem like too much to handle."

Becky sat there, trying to think of how to word her reply. Her mother was acting as though she was on the verge of a nervous breakdown or something when nothing all that world-shaking was happening. "Mom, I'm okay. Nothing's bothering me, believe me. Nothing except not getting enough sleep and my crazy, mixed-up schedule."

"I know exactly what you mean," her mother sighed. "The crazy, mixed-up schedule was one of the things that made me give up skating. That and meeting your father, of course. We got married. I got pregnant with you . . ." She stopped, shrugged, and said self-deprecatingly, "You know, I've been reciting that old routine so long, even *I'm* beginning to believe it. No, the schedule wasn't it. And it wasn't meeting your father, either. I was afraid, that was why I gave it up. Afraid of the pressure, the competition, afraid that, if I tried and failed, I wouldn't be able to cope."

Becky searched her mother's eyes. "Was that *really* it? Mom, that's just like *me*. That's exactly how I feel. That if I don't make it to the Olympics, I won't be able to handle it."

Her mother reached for her hand. "That's what's bothering you, isn't it? Lovey, you know how much I want this for you — almost as much as you want it for yourself. But as much as it means to both of us, it's not worth your health or happiness. The day it becomes too much for you to handle, that'll be the day you'll stop competing. At sixteen, with all your other talents, there are a lot of options . . ."

"Yeah, like college?" Becky said, dropping her eyes. "Uh, uh, Mom. For me there's only one thing, and that's the skating. And I won't stop competing, no matter what. One thing I don't think I could live with, and that's having to say to myself someday, 'I could have made it to the Olympics, but I copped out and didn't try.' I'd rather live with *anything* than that!"

She glanced up. Her father stood in the doorway, looking sleepy and rumpled, peering in at them from behind his hair. "I knew it! I told you, didn't I, Sara? But you wouldn't listen. And now she's sick. We'd better phone Marshall Arlen right away."

"He's already been here, Daddy, and he said there's nothing wrong with me, that I'm healthy as a horse."

"He thinks she's picked up something," Becky's mother said, trying to calm him down with the tone of her voice. "He says to keep her in bed a day or two, just to be on the safe side. Alex, don't get hysterical. It's just a little virus. She'll be fine by tomorrow."

"I'd better be," Becky said, scrunching down in bed. "I'm going to a party tomorrow night!" She lay there, blinking up at them, flabbergasted. Where had *that* come from? Until this moment she had had no intention whatsoever of going to Chrissy Raines's party. How and when had she changed her mind? And why hadn't she been aware of having changed it?

"A *what*?" Her mother was staring at her as though she had just announced her intention to join the next expedition to outer space.

"Mom, take it easy, will you? I won't go unless I'm totally better, and if I do go, I'll only stay 'til ten or ten-thirty at the latest. I promise. Really."

Her mother shook her head in disbelief. "All I

can say is you certainly are a bundle of contradictions today."

"A bundle of contradictions? Because I want to go to a party? Maybe the very last party of my whole high school career, and a Christmas party too? But don't you see? A party's exactly what I need. Some recreation. Something besides skating all the time. Something that's fun instead of work, work, work!"

"Oh, what a con job!"

"Mom, you know what? It's been so long since I did anything normal, like an average American teenager, you've forgotten what an average American teenager is!"

"She should go," Becky's father cried, rushing into the fray. "Isn't that what being young is all about, going out and having fun?"

"You could've fooled me," Becky muttered.

Her mother broke it up. "All right, all right, go! But Daddy and I are picking you up. No, don't argue. The movie's over at ten-twenty. We'll be there around ten-thirty, a quarter to eleven."

"Oh, Mom!" Becky groaned.

"Ten-thirty *is* a little on the early side," her father said. He shot her a conspiratorial smile, and when her mother was out of earshot, added, "Be young while you can, Beanie. Believe me, it's a whole lot harder when you're older."

"My, Daddy, what a profound insight!"

He blushed and grinned. "Well, it is when you think about it," he said, heading for the door. He turned back, his finger on his lips. "Maybe I can talk Mom into going somewhere for a drink or something after the movie."

CHAPTER TEN

"Are you still among the living?" Dee collapsed into the rocker, kicked off her shoes, and wriggled her toes in the carpet. "Oh, my feet! I swear, one of these days I'm going to throw those skates away and never set foot on the ice again as long as I live! How do you feel? You look kind of *bluchy*. What did the doctor say was wrong with you?"

"Nothing. I'm supposedly healthy as a horse. So if I'm so healthy, why do I feel like warmed-over meat loaf?" She lowered her voice, just in case her mother was anywhere in the near vicinity. "Remember I told you about that case Ms. Wing told us about, the girl who was paralyzed from the neck down?"

"Yeah. So? Now you're gonna tell me that's why you're lying there feeling like warmed-over meat loaf? Because you're paralyzed from the neck down?'"

"Dopey, the girl's problem was all psychological. She wasn't really paralyzed. She just thought she was. See, she was looking for attention, and that's the way she got it. The whole thing was psychosomatic. A psychosomatic illness."

"Didn't I tell you not to elect that psych class? It's really messing up your head. Now I suppose you'll tell me the reason you're lying there like warmed-over meat loaf is you're looking for attention. Beck, you've got too much attention as it is! Anyway, you're not the type. Anyone who knows anything about psychology would know that."

She fished up several balled-up pieces of notebook paper from her bookbag and put them on the nighttable beside the bed. "Here. I brought you your homework assignments. Mr. Ormsby sends his regards and says he hopes you get better soon. Mrs. Finkel says you'll have to take a makeup test for the one you missed today. Ms. Wing says get better quick, the class isn't the same without you, and Sean Mercer sends his undying love and wants to know is there anything he can do for you. And I *don't* think he meant make chicken soup! What's with him anyway? Has he got a crush on you?"

"Sean Mercer? Mr. Male Chauvinist, with whom I played Spin the Bottle back in fifth grade? Dee, don't be ludicrous!"

Dee took the wad of gum from her mouth, wrapped it in a piece of scrap paper, dumped it in the wastebasket, and started in on a fresh pack. "You played Spin the Bottle with Jed too, once, and now look," she laughed. "Listen, I need your advice about something. I've been wracking my brain, trying to come up with something sensational to wear to the party, and the only thing I can think of is my purple velour dress. What d'you think?"

"I think nobody'll be wearing a dress."

"Exactly why I want to wear one!" She went on waxing eloquent about how crucial it was to be an individual, someone original with a style of your own, not one of the crowd, while Becky sat there, waiting to drop the proverbial bomb. After you'd spent weeks and weeks delivering endless soap-box orations on the importance of staying in training, it was rather embarrassing to suddenly announce you were going to break it yourself at the first opportunity. Finally, when Dee started to wind down and she could get a word in, she blurted, "Dee, I'm going to the party!" Dee's eyebrows flew up. She sat there for a minute, staring at her, then burst out laughing.

"I must say, it is a huge relief to find out you're a human being after all and not a computerized skating machine traveling incognito." Dee took her hair pick out of her bookbag and started poking at her hair, watching herself in the mirror across the room.

75

"Well, now that you've decided to join the human race, we'll have to figure out something smashing for you to wear. You could borrow something of mine if you want to. My new paper-bag trousers? The red velvet baggies with the suspenders? The black satin overalls with the vest and the bowtie?"

"I was thinking about jeans," Becky offered.

"Jeans? Well, really. How tacky! How *très, très ordinaire*, as dear Mater would say. Honestly, you'd think she was the one who was French, not my father. She's got more of an accent than he does. Well, if you're going to insist on jeans, at least wear the *Chemin de Fers*, not your tacky Levis. And the pink shirt I gave you last Christmas. Now how about shoes? Have you got anything besides sneakers and those horrendous hiking boots?"

"My Fryes."

"Fryes? Beck, this is a party, not a street rumble. You'll look like a linebacker from the Los Angeles Rams. What about those platform thingees your mother got you for your cousin's wedding? Why can't you wear those?"

"Oh, right. I forgot about them. Do they go with jeans, though?"

"Darling, *everything* goes with jeans. You dumbhead, don't you ever read the fashion magazines?"

Becky grabbed one of her pillows and threw it at Dee's head. "Read the fashion magazines? I don't even have time to sleep, and she wants me to read fashion magazines. Okay, check. *Chemin de Fers*, pink Christmas shirt, which I adore with a mad passion, by the way, and el wedding shoes-ios. So tell me, Calvin Klein, am I dressed yet? Hey, a party! Me, Becky B., going to a real party with music and people and dancing and everything. Isn't that a gas? Aren't we excited?"

"Oh, madly!" Dee rummaged in her bookbag, came up with a half an emery board and began filing her nails. "Uh, lemme see. There's still something missing, that indefinable *quelque chose très chic*, as my father would say. That special thing that makes an outfit *an outfit*. How about the black satin vest your mom made you for your birthday? I'm not sure how it'll look with the shirt, but try it and see."

"Check and doublecheck. I don't know what I'd do without you, my own private fashion consultant."

"Listen, someday when I'm a wealthy, world-famous fashion designer with showrooms in Paris, London, and New York, you can tell everyone you knew me when."

"You'll be one too. Bet on it."

"*Mais oui.* Of course," Dee chortled, throwing the emery board in the air, leaping out of the rocker and prancing around the room. She glanced at the clock. "Hey, lookit the time, will you? I've got to split. Mater's away at the milk farm, starving herself for the sake of feminine bee-oo-tee, and Delia and Deena both have dates, so *Papa* is taking *Bebe* out for Chinese food. I was supposed to meet him at Wing Ho's an hour ago. Honestly, he's so chauvinistic, it's incredible. He wouldn't boil himself an egg if he was on the verge of starvation. If you even suggest he make a pot of coffee, he's incensed. I can't understand how the man manages to stay so unliberated with me for a daughter, can you? I mean, haven't I tried to raise his consciousness? Haven't I attempted to enlighten his mind? Didn't I even go out and buy him a copy of *The Feminine Mystique* for his birthday?"

Becky watched Dee jam her size fives into her spike-heeled clogs, retrieve the emery board from under the bed, and gather up her things. "Hey, did you ever really read that book?"

Dee shook her head. "No, but I know every single word in it. Listen, I meant to ask you. Does Jed know you're going to a party tomorrow night?"

"Not unless he's telepathic."

"Oh, good! I suggest you don't tell him. When a person's as crazy-wild about a person as Jed Hollander is about you, and is five hundred miles away from that person, it's often wise to dispense with such questionable information."

Becky burst out laughing. "Dee, Jed's not uptight about that sort of thing, not in the least. And he's not even mildly jealous or possessive. You know that. How could you know him all this time and not? I don't know. Sometimes you're just so, well, inconsistent. One minute you're putting your father down for being chauvinistic. The next *you're* being chauvinistic. You keep saying how totally liberated you are, but you insist it's necessary for you to play mind games with Danny Pharaoh to keep him interested. You say you can live without boys, that they're not all that important to you, but you've always got to have at least one boyfriend hanging around, adoring you with his eyes. Make up your mind, will you? Liberated or unliberated? Which is it?"

Dee picked up her sheepskin jacket and her bookbag and started out of the room, sending Becky a tantalizingly mysterious smile over her shoulder. "A little of both, *ma chere*," she called as she went down the hall. "I'm me, Deirdre Marie Lisette Danziger, a gorgeous, talented, charming, witty, exceedingly lovable, seventeen-year-old *woman*. I'm, well, I'm the way I am, that's all. I'm not going to change, so take it or leave it!"

Becky listened to the sound of her high heels clunking away down the stairs. "I'll take it!" she called as they clicked across the parquet floor of the front entryway. "I wouldn't want you to change. Not one iota!"

Her mother insisted on bringing her dinner up on a tray.

"Mom, you're spoiling me. I'm not all that sick," Becky said, tucking the napkin under her chin. She commenced to attack a piece of broiled chicken, amazed to discover that along with the last vestiges of her stomachache she also had a voracious appetite. Her mother sat down in the rocker right on top of Ronald Bear. She jumped up, grabbed him, put him on the bed, and sat down again, reaching to break a tiny piece from Becky's buttered roll, sticking it in her mouth before she had time to change her mind.

"This reminds me of when you were little," she said, munching ecstatically. "I used to think you got sick on purpose so I'd make a fuss over you. What a wonderful baby you were! So good, so beautiful."

"Beautiful? Mom, you're blocking. I was a fat slob!"

"You, a fat slob? Don't be silly! You were beautiful. Everybody said so. Even when you were first born, you were beautiful. When the doctor handed you to me, and I saw that adorable little nose, those round, pink cheeks, that tuft of blonde hair sticking straight up, I thought to myself, 'She's special!' And I was right. You were. And are." She laughed, looking a little embarrassed, and added, "Not my style, getting corny and nostalgic, is it? Well, it must be old age creeping up on me, I guess." She stood up and started for the door, throwing Becky a smile over her shoulder. "I've got Chicken Kiev in the oven and a martini warming on the counter. My only offspring is sick, you see, and my husband and I are taking this rare opportunity to have a romantic, candlelit dinner alone together."

"Ah, how sweet!"

"Yes, well, if you want anything, yell, but not too loud please. I don't break my diet on Chicken Kiev every day of the week. Oh, I spoke to Marsh Arlen, and we've decided you're to stay home one more day, just in case. He says you couldn't skate right after being sick, anyway."

Becky put down her roll. "I can't stay home, Mom. You know that. I can't take two days off right before an exhibition."

"Doctor's orders," her mother said from the doorway. "One more day. Think of it as insurance."

"Insurance," Becky muttered, sticking her spoon in the middle of her jello to make it shimmy. "Insurance like that I could cheerfully live without! Let's face it, even Dorothy Hamill never took out *that* kind of insurance two days before an exhibition."

She finished her dinner, put the tray on the nighttable, and started checking out her homework assignments. When she heard two sets of footsteps coming up the stairs, she assumed it was her parents and started to offer a compromise solution, like maybe skating *one* session the following day. Her mother came into the room, wearing that too-cheerful smile she always wore when she was just the opposite of cheerful. Thundering into the room behind her was Vera, wearing the picturesque mouton coat and a hat like a Russian cossack.

"Are vee sick, or are vee faking?" she said, descending on Becky, a grim look on her face.

"The doctor thinks she may have picked up some kind of virus," Becky's mother offered in a meek voice.

Becky made her eyelids droop languidly. "I felt pretty bad yesterday, but I feel a lot better now." She hoped she sounded convincing. She stole a look at Vera's face. Why did she feel so guilty? She was really sick, wasn't she? Vera had this way of looking at you that made you feel guilty when you had nothing to feel guilty about, as though you had committed some crime too heinous to mention in mixed company. Did Vera really believe she was faking, even after all the times she had shown up at the rink to skate with colds, viruses, the flu, and once even pneumonia?

Vera lowered her girth into the rocker. It was way too small for her, and parts of her kind of oozed out the sides. She began to rock, pushing off with her enormous fur boots. Becky wondered idly, if Vera kept on rocking long enough, would she ultimately rock her way all the way through to the basement?

"I haff brought you somethink," Vera said, taking a bottle of evil-looking stuff from her satchel and setting it down on the nighttable. "Two tablespoonsz every four hoursz, yes?"

"What's in it?" Becky inquired, eyeing the bottle.

"Natur-ull ingredientsz. Nothink ar-tee-fish-ull. Herbsz only, und vegetablesz. Und fish oilsz to help you ree-siszt germsz."

"I'll go get a spoon," gulped Becky's mother, looking as though she was about to wretch.

"Coward!" thought Becky, staring balefully after her.

Vera laid the back of one huge, sandpapery paw against her forehead. "Goot! No feifer. So! The other day, ven you vere havink your leszon, skatink like a beginner, you vere really gettink sick. Vera, she shouldt haff known, yes? Now Rebecca, you must not vorry. If you do not feel vellenuf, you do not haff to skate in the exhibition on Sunday." She laughed at the shocked look on Becky's face and added, "Tell me, are you eatink right? You must keep up your strength. Vera, she iss goink to bake you some cookiesz. Ah, you are surprisze-et? You did not think Vera, she coudt cook. But I tell you a secret, chust betwveen you und me. Vera, she iss takink cookink lessonsz, und someday, ven she iss gettink too olt to teach, she iss goink to open a restaurant. A Hungarian restaurant. Then you vill come, und Vera, she vill make you goulash like you haff never tastedt in your life."

"I've never tasted goulash, Vera."

"Never tastedt goulash?" Vera exclaimed, as though Becky had just confessed she'd never learned to do a figure eight. "Vell, now you vill haff somethink to vich to look forwardt, Hungarian goulash a la Vera! Ha, ha, ha." Still laughing, a thing Becky couldn't remember ever having heard her do before, she hauled herself out of the rocker and stampeded across the room and out the door.

"What did she have to say?" Becky's mother asked, coming back upstairs a little while later with tea and cinnamon toast on a tray.

"She said she was going to bake me some cookies."

"Oh? That's nice!"

"And that someday, when she's too old to teach, she's going to open a restaurant. One mit *goulash*."

"A restaurant? Vera? I didn't even know she could cook."

"And that if I didn't feel up to it, I didn't have to skate in the exhibition."

"Vera said that?" her mother exclaimed. "Are you sure? Maybe you were hallucinating. Well, I'm relieved. I wasn't looking forward to doing battle with her in case you weren't well enough. You won't believe this, but she scares me!"

"Join the club!" Becky pointed to the bottle on the nighttable. "I don't have to take that, do I? Maybe I ought to rub it into my sore leg."

Her mother picked up the bottle, holding it

way out in front of her as though she thought it might bite. "I shall dispose of it," she said, starting from the room.

"Mom? I'm not going to miss that exhibition, you know."

"You are if you're not all better," her mother replied, going off down the stairway, her Fryes drumming a muted accompaniment on the carpet.

"Okay, Mom. You win. I'll stay in all day tomorrow, even though there's really nothing wrong with me, and rest until I'm blue in the face. But, unless I'm *dying*, I'm skating on Sunday." She paused, then added in a louder voice, "And I'm going to that party, Mom." There was a long moment of stunned silence as her mother reacted to that one. Becky could almost hear her reacting, carefully framing an appropriate reply. "Mom? Did you hear what I said? *I am going to that party!*"

"I heard," her mother called after another pause, "but for the sake of my own sanity, I've decided to ignore you."

CHAPTER
ELEVEN

"Who wants breakfast?" Her father poked his head in her door bright and early next morning, looking sleepy and scruffy, needing a shave. Her mother was right behind him, looking totally together, as though she had just come from the beauty parlor. She was dressed up like a cowgirl in skin-tight Levis, a checkered Western shirt, a leather vest, and Fryes.

"Did a hurricane blow through here, or are you just doing your spring cleaning early?" she said, looking around the room with a horrified expression.

"I was just going to straighten up," Becky lied, leaping out of bed. She gathered up the clothes and things that littered the floor and the chairbacks, semi-straightened her dresser and desktop, pulled the bed together, and followed her parents downstairs. Her father was whipping up his specialty, French toast. She waited for Northridge's answer to the French Chef to finish creating, then made herself two poached eggs on wholewheat toast.

"She's still sick!" her father said when he saw what she was eating.

"Daddy, a person doesn't have to be sick to eat poached eggs on toast for breakfast. You're allowed to eat poached eggs on toast even when you're not sick. I eat poached eggs on toast very often. That is because I happen to love poached eggs on toast." She became intent on spearing the egg yolks so that they would ooze out evenly over the toast, hoping they would drop the subject. For the hundredth time in a row her mother felt her forehead for fever.

"You could have a relapse, you know," she said.

Becky put down her fork. "I could also fall down an open manhole, step on a live wire, get in the path of a falling airplane. A lot of awful things could happen to me. Maybe you'd like me to spend the rest of my life locked up in the storage closet, along with the sterling and the good china. That way I'd *really* be safe." She got busy mopping up egg yolk, half-expecting them to continue the hassle, but, oddly enough, they didn't. She was so grateful, she got completely carried away and offered to clean up. "I owe you guys one, remember? For the other night?"

She was up to her elbows in dirty dishes when the phone rang.

"Hiya, Blades. It's me, your long-lost lover."

"Jed! Gosh, you sound funny. Have you got a cold?"

"Yeah, a three-week cold. By this time it's verging on double pneumonia."

"Did you see a doctor?"

"Um hum. She said I needed love."

Becky laughed. "Well, you'll get plenty of that if you're coming down next weekend. You *are* coming down, aren't you? Sixteen relatives phoned us to ask if they could come, but we told them no, the guest room was already reserved."

"I'll be there," Jed said between coughs. "If I have to spend one more weekend up here, I'll go bonkers. Listen, let's catch a flick Saturday night. It's been ages since I've seen a flick."

"You, the movie fanatic? Okay, but we'll have to make the early show, because until the end of March the early session at the rink starts at seven on weekends."

"Seven! Listen, tell Rick to stop undermining my love life."

"It wasn't Rick's idea. It was the parents, all except mine, of course. They got together and coerced him into changing the schedule. They said it interfered with their weekends."

"Terrific! A ten o'clock curfew wasn't bad enough. Now it'll be nine."

"Well, who told you to fall in love with a

skater? Oh, I almost forgot. Dee says I shouldn't tell you, but I have this irresistable urge to confess all. I'm going to a party tonight."

"You? Compulsive Cora? Going to a party the night before an exhibition? You've got to be putting me on!"

"Well, it's a Christmas party, probably the last party of my senior year, so I figure I ought to go. You know, the whole nostalgia trip."

"Yeah, like I did last year, remember? By the way, I got the job at Lake Placid for the summer. It's all set. I don't know how I'll survive until then. It's a bummer, keeping up with the schoolwork and the part-time job. The professors up here are merciless, especially on us scholarship students. Kids are dropping out like flies, and the ones who're left are so cutthroat, you think you're on Wall Street, not a college campus. Listen, I almost forgot the reason I spent my hard-earned money calling you. Good luck in the exhibition tomorrow. Do you realize this'll be the first exhibition in six years you'll be skating without me?"

"I know. I was just saying that to Mom the other day. I wish you could be here. You always bring me good luck. I was checking out my calendar, and you know what? It's been six weeks since we saw each other. Six weeks! That's the longest we've been apart since that time you went to Maine to summer camp when we were in sixth grade, remember?"

"Is he coming down, or isn't he?" her father asked, coming into the kitchen just as she was hanging up the phone.

"He's coming."

"How's he doing up there? Is he still working? How're his grades?"

"Not so hot, he says, but you know Jed. To him not so hot means an A instead of an A-plus."

"That's the way it goes when you're a bona fide boy genius!" Her father rolled up his sleeves and plunged his hands into the sink. "I decided to take pity on you and give you a hand."

"Aha! And just the other day you were chastising Mom for not being consistent."

He rinsed off a dish and put it in the dishwasher. "To tell the truth, I wanted to hear what Jed had to say and if he was still planning on coming. Guess you're not the only one in this family who misses him."

Becky got dressed and went to check herself out in the mirror. She wasn't sure she liked the outfit all that much. Dee was right. Jeans *were* tacky. She wished she had something new and smashing to wear.

Her parents picked Dee up, and they got to Chrissy's around a quarter to eight.

"Don't forget, we're picking you up," her mother called as the two girls headed up Chrissy's front walk.

Dee didn't say anything, but Becky could tell

90

she was anything but thrilled. "My father's going to try and get her to go out for a drink or something after the movie. They probably won't get here 'til eleven. Parties always make me nervous," she said, jabbing the front doorbell with her index finger. "Especially the first part when you just walk in and don't know what to expect."

"You're just out of practice," Dee said, bending to adjust the strap of her sandal. "The last time you went to a party was nineteen-seventy!"

Chrissy opened the door. When she saw Becky, she broke into a big grin. "Becky, you changed your mind! Or was the exhibition called off?"

"You were right the first time. I hope you don't mind my just showing up without letting you know."

"What's to mind? Downstairs there are three-hundred stampeding elephants on the loose. I don't know *half* of them. You, you're a friend!" She took their jackets and ushered them downstairs. The noise was so deafening, they had to scream to be heard.

"Welcome to Studio Fifty-Four!" Dee shouted in Becky's ear.

Becky had never seen anything like it. The room was a real discotheque, complete with strobe lights, a sound booth, mirrors on the walls and ceiling, the works. There were a bunch of kids boogying to Bee Gees tunes. The strobe lights made them all look spastic. Across the room was a buffet table loaded with all kinds of scrumptious-looking food. Sean Mercer was behind the bar, making like a bartender, wearing this dumb-looking straw hat and passing out sodas.

"I thought you weren't coming," he said when Becky walked over.

"I changed my mind," she replied, accepting a Coke. Dee started to boogy away in the direction of the food to see if there was anything worth breaking her diet on, which left Becky to contend with Sean and his eyes. She sipped her Coke, surreptitiously checking out the action. Danny Pharaoh came in and made an immediate beeline for Dee. Dee was piling egg salad on a slab of pumpernickel. She took a bite, then fed the rest to Danny. They stood close together, sharing egg salad on pumpernickel, a couple of lovebirds. Becky felt a pang of self-pity. She wished Jed was here. She really felt like a fifth wheel.

Sue Farber arrived, hanging on to the arm of a tall, redheaded boy. Chrissy's seventeen-year-old brother Bobby walked in with some of his friends. Becky knew Bobby Raines. In fact, she knew most of the kids at the party, had known them all her life almost. So there was no reason for her to feel uptight or self-conscious. Still she did. Very.

Lee Marks sidled over, smirking at her. Lee had always been one of her least-favorite people, ever since kindergarten, when he had spent the year teasing her about her height. Unlike a lot of the other boys she had grown up with, Lee didn't improve with age. In fact, just the opposite.

Somebody put on a Beatles tape. Dee came boogying over, looking kind of chagrined for some reason. "Beck, Danny's driving me home, okay?" Before Becky could say a word, she danced away again, stopping for a couple of seconds of fancy footwork. She was a terrific dancer, a real disco queen. When she was on the floor, even the pros looked like amateurs.

"Wanna dance?" Sean grabbed Becky, pulled her on to the floor, then started doing all these fancy maneuvers, acting as though he thought he was the world's greatest dancer. Becky ignored him and did her own thing. It was nothing new, dancing all alone. She did it all the time at home in front of her mirrors. "Why don't we go upstairs, huh?" Sean said in a husky voice she supposed he thought was sexy, but which sounded a lot like laryngitis or croup to her. His hand started to explore her back.

"Would you *mind*?" she said, peeling it away.

Lee stood on the edge of the floor watching them. "Mercer, forget it. You'll never score with that chick. She's a real deep freeze. You know what the guys call her: The Ice Princess."

Becky stopped dancing. Sean kept on going. "Hey, come on," he said, leering at her. "Don't get shook, man. It's no big thing. Everybody's got a nickname, even me."

"Really, Sean? What's yours, *the slime*?" She

93

strode off, leaving him on the dance floor, dancing all by himself, looking idiotic. Maybe she was being paranoiac, but she didn't like finding out that she had been the subject of Lee and Sean's locker-room conversation. Anyway, she felt so out of it at this party, like an outsider nobody liked or accepted. She knew darned well all the kids thought she was stuck-up, a real snob. It wasn't that at all, but she'd never be able to *prove* it to them. She knew better than to try.

She felt so disappointed. She had wanted to come to this party so badly she had practically jeopardized the most important exhibition of the year, and now she was winding up having the world's worst time. Honestly, she wished she had listened to her mother and stayed home!

Across the room Lee and Sean had their heads together, looking over at her and sniggering. She felt herself blushing. There was nothing like being the one grasshopper among a multitude of ants, was there? Well, she'd just go upstairs, that's all, and find a place to hide out in until it was time to go home. She should have known better than to think she'd enjoy herself at a dumb old kids' party, anyway.

She found a room with a lot of plants in it, flopped down in a chair, picked up a magazine, and began to read. Well, here she was, alone again, as usual. It was pretty depressing. A guest at the orgy of the century, and what did she wind up doing? Barricading herself in a plant-infested room and reading a magazine. What a swinger *she* was!

"Did you have a good time?" her mother asked when she climbed into the car.

"No, I had a cruddy time. The party was a crashing bore, Lee Marks was his usual obnoxious self, Sean Mercer made a pass, and I spent practically the entire evening upstairs in the Raines's greenhouse, being stared at by a group of very menacing-looking plants. A really thrilling evening, that's what it was. And after all I went through to go, it just isn't fair! I would've been better off staying home, or going to the movies with you guys."

"Ah, the perils of early maturity," Becky's father exclaimed in his Shakespearean-actor's voice.

"And what's *that* supposed to mean?"

He grinned at her in the rearview mirror. "It means that it's difficult when you're sixteen going on thirty, and all your peers are just sixteen."

CHAPTER
TWELVE

She woke with the usual pre-performance stomachache. "I intend to ignore you, stomach," she said, heading for the shower, "so you might as well just go away."

She showered, did her hair, and got dressed. At six-thirty she dialed Dee's private number. "Are you awake? I was afraid you'd oversleep, so I thought I'd better call you. What time did you finally get home?"

"Early. Danny and I had this enormous fight, and I made him bring me home. I don't know how I ever thought I could like him. What a creep! Just because we've gone out a few times, he thinks I'll let him do whatever he feels like doing. Listen, what're you wearing today? I'm wearing my white. I was planning on wearing my black, but *chere Maman*, the fashion expert, insists it's too sophisticated, and that the judges'll get turned off." She rambled on and on, talking endlessly, skipping from one subject to another without taking a breath, really wound up. She was always nervous before a performance. She shouldn't have been today, though. This wasn't a real competition or anything. They weren't going to be judged or rated, just watched by the eagle eyes of three Olympic Committee judges. That wasn't exactly like skating the Christmas Ice Pageant for your friends and neighbors at Northridge Rink, but it wasn't a National competition, either.

"Dee, I've got to go," Becky said when Dee began to wind down. "I'll see you there, okay? Please don't be late, and remember—no gumchewing!"

She could almost *hear* Dee waiting, her apprehension traveling the telephone wires. "Listen, don't be nervous, okay? Because it's no big deal. Anyway, you're one-half of the world's most stupendous figure skating team, The Dynamic Duo, The Best on Blades. Just skate half as well as you did last time, and they'll be giving you a standing ovation."

"Sure, a standing ovation," Dee said and hung up. Becky went to take one last look in the mirror. The girl in the mirror didn't look much like that skinny, tired girl who worked out there every morning in leotards and leg warmers. She didn't like to sound conceited, but she felt beautiful in the filmy mauve chiffon dress with its wisp of a skirt like a ballerina's, its narrow satin ribbons wound around and around the waist, the cap sleeves that looked like an angel's wings. She had put her hair up on top of her head, fastening it with two flowered combs, allowing a few stray tendrils to escape and curl around her ears, her forehead, and the back of her neck. The hairdo made her look even more like a ballerina.

She gave one last tug at the waistband of the dress and headed downstairs. She had no appetite, but she forced herself to eat some hot cereal for energy and to help calm her stomach. Breakfast was uncharacteristically solemn and silent. No fun and games like on usual mornings. Her parents were pretty nervous, too. Her father kept jiggling his foot up and down, drumming on the table with his fingers. It drove her crazy. Luckily her mother's nervousness exhibited itself in another, more tolerable, way. She just got real quiet and kind of retreated into herself and didn't come out until whatever it was that was making her nervous was over.

The drive into the city seemed to take six times longer than usual. Becky sat huddled under the car blanket in the back seat, pretending to be looking out the window, the usual hysteria mounting by leaps and bounds. The same old horrifying thoughts kept popping into her head.

What if the ice hadn't been resurfaced properly and was all gravelly and bumpy, or worse, overly wet and slick? What if her dress ripped right in the middle of her performance? What if her skate laces snapped? What if she goofed on the new jump-spin, fell, hurt herself, or got sick in the middle of the piece and had to be taken off the ice on a stretcher? How had she ever allowed herself to be talked into taking off two days just before an important exhibition like this? Was she out of her mind completely? Temporarily deranged? Everyone knew how crucially important those two days were.

They pulled into the underground parking lot. Her mother turned to her with a smile. "Calm down. You're going to be fine. You needed the rest. If anything, you'll skate better, not worse."

Vera was waiting for them inside, pacing back and forth like a caged lion, looking like one too in a big shaggy coat. Becky hurried to put on her skates, anxious to get in as much practice time as possible before the performance. She headed out on to the ice, too preoccupied with her own thoughts to notice John Verucci, the rink pro, waving to her from the other side of the rink.

She began the stroking. Six strokes on the straightaway, three progressives on the turns. Coming into the third turn she was grinning to herself. She was skating beautifully, better than she had in months. It just proved what her mother was always saying. Sometimes, when you got overpracticed and overworked, it paid to take a little time off, get some distance and a fresh perspective on your work. When you came back, you were skating better.

Skating sure was a mysterious process. Even Vera, the all-knowing, admitted she didn't understand how it worked, so how could Becky, the unknowing?

She promised herself to learn from this experience and file the information away for future reference. It was good to know that when things got sticky you could give in to yourself a little and not suffer dire consequences. Knowing herself, though, she'd probably forget this the next time and get hysterical all over again.

Dee showed up at about nine, only a half hour late, pretty good for Dee. She looked sensational in her new white silk dress with its silver-sequined vest and her silver skates.

"That dress is to die from!" she said, skating over to Becky. "Your mom's the most talented person. She ought to be doing this professionally. Bet she'd make a mint. When my mother sees that dress, she'll be green with envy. She paid a fortune for this one, and it doesn't come near yours."

"Isn't that Jojo Starbuck over there?" Becky whispered, purposely changing the subject. A pretty blonde woman had come in on the arm of a big, tall guy in a sheepskin jacket. "That's her husband, Terry Bradshaw. He's a football player. Isn't that Peggy Fleming over there? Wow, Sky's crawling with celebrities today."

"Sky's always crawling with celebrities," Dee replied, acting blasé. "Don't get carried away. They're just people, like us."

"Well, not exactly like us. There are a few differences. For instance, we don't earn thousands skating in ice shows."

The bleachers were filling up fast. She recognized a couple of well-known TV and movie stars, a television talk-show host, some semi-famous athletes and newspaper people. A camera crew came in and started setting up at rinkside, and her stomach rolled over and played dead. Even after all these years, she wasn't used to this. Knowing the cameras were there made her so self-conscious; not like Dee who adored being on camera and really knew what to do when the cameras were rolling.

"Come on," Becky said, yanking Dee's arm, "we'd better get off the ice. I feel like a *nerd* standing here in front of everybody."

Vera was ensconced on the bench, the fur coat draped over her knees. She bundled them into their jackets and started issuing a long list of instructions. Becky was only half-listening. She'd heard the whole pre-performance lecture a thousand times before and knew it by heart. She scanned the bleachers. The judges, two men and a woman, were sitting there stony-faced, staring straight ahead of them as though they were afraid that if they looked in the direction of any particular skater they'd be accused of favoritism.

The rink manager finally skated out to make the usual announcements: the names of the skaters, their clubs, their backgrounds, their pros, etc. Becky began to fidget. This was the part she hated. She wished he'd get it over with so they could get on with the performances.

Someone in the bleachers behind her said, "There's that Bacall girl, the one in the purple dress."

"It's not purple. It's mauve," she thought, her face getting hot. Her stomach was making these weird noises, and her hands and feet had turned to ice. Her breath kept getting caught in her chest, making her wheeze noisily. Vera heard her wheezing and shot her a look. "Don't worry," Becky said. "I'm just doing my biofeedback breathing."

"Sure you are," Dee muttered under her breath. "You're just having a quiet nervous breakdown."

The first bars of *Swan Lake* came over the loudspeaker. Dee looked at Becky, and Becky looked away to keep from laughing. The first skater skated out, a girl from Westchester named Allison Saunders. Becky had met her a few times in regional competitions. She was good, a skilled and well-trained skater, considering her age, but not a particularly dynamic or stylish one. She was fourteen, a little pudgy, still lacking the maturity, polish, and professionalism of older skaters. She started off well, skating adequately but not brilliantly. Halfway through the piece she goofed on a double axel and fell, and from then on she skated badly.

"What a *klutz*!" Dee whispered.

"She's not really." Becky felt sorry for Allison. She knew how it felt to fall during a performance. You told yourself not to clutch, that it could happen to anyone, and to make the rest of the performance as good as you possibly could. But no matter what you told yourself, a fall was a fall and pretty demoralizing. Even the best, most professional, and experienced skaters tended to skate badly after taking a fall.

Allison finished her piece, skated off, collapsed on the bench and burst into tears. Her pro came over, sat down next to her and put his arm around her shoulder. Becky glanced over at Vera. She was watching the scene with a disapproving expression. She believed in stoicism at all times. Emotions weren't allowed. She never would have let one of her pupils indulge in an emotional free-for-all like that.

The second skater was a boy named Leslie Sokol. Becky had met him the year before at Lake Placid. He was a new pupil of John Verucci's whose family had moved to the East from the Midwest somewhere so Leslie could study with John. He was wearing this skin-tight, black jumpsuit that showed off his terrific physique.

"What a hunk!" Dee whispered. Throughout

103

Leslie's performance she sat there fidgeting, chomping away on the ever-present wad of gum, making weird faces, fiddling with her hair, tying and retying her skate laces, and squirming around on the bench. Anyone watching her would have thought she had some kind of nervous problem, she was so hyper.

"Are you okay?" Becky said.

"Don't I look okay?"

"Of course you don't look okay! How can you ask me that question?"

Dee gave her a look and went back to fidgeting. When her name was called, she stood up, looking as though she was going to pass out any second. Then she stepped out on to the ice and underwent the usual transformation — from complete nervous hysteric to calm, cool, and collected professional. Becky grinned to herself. She could never figure out how or why Dee did it, but she did it every time. Becky had given up worrying about it long ago.

Dee was skating to an old Beatles tune, "Norwegian Wood." The piece began with a complicated series of jumps and spins. Dee excelled at jumps and spins, and today she went through them as though she were taking a walk around the block, not skating an exhibition. There was only one thing she ever had trouble with, and that was the Russian split. Of course she did it whenever possible, even though Vera kept begging her not to. Becky just prayed the split would go off okay.

Dee's performance was so terrific so far, it would have been a shame to ruin it now.

Dee cleared the ice, lifting high into the air, legs extended, fingers touching her toes. She touched down, light as air, and immediately went into the lay back spin. The audience applauded appreciatively. Becky glanced at Vera. She was smiling.

Dee finished the piece and began to stroke off. As she passed the judges, she stopped, dimpled up, and threw a kiss to the audience. She made it look so spontaneous. Who would have guessed she had been rehearsing it for weeks and weeks?

"You big cornball!" Becky giggled.

"Was I all right?" Dee whispered, collapsing on the bench.

"All right? Listen to that applause. You were brilliant!" She glanced over at the judges. Two out of the three were smiling, both of them men.

As the next skater skated out, Becky began her breathing. She closed her eyes, and started counting breaths, filling her lungs with air, holding it to the count of thirty, letting the air out a little at a time. *"Easy does it. That's my girl,"* she said to herself. She always did the breathing just before a performance. It relaxed her, gave her extra energy, increased her circulation, and helped her to concentrate.

When she heard her name over the loudspeaker, she left the bench, smiling (by now at least *that* was automatic), and skated to the center of the rink. Her music began, and she glided forward, accomplishing the first series of movements with her usual precision timing, grace, and style. She began the turning moves preparatory to the new jump-spin, taking it slow and easy, the timer inside her head telling her exactly when to make each move. She lifted off, rising into the air, spinning, touching down so lightly her blades hardly made a whisper on the ice. There was a burst of applause. She went into the attitude finish. The audience rose to its feet, applauding wildly. She held the position, relishing the sound of the applause. This was it, her moment. This was what made it all worthwhile. This was where it all came together, all the dedication, hard work, and sacrifice, in a performance so flawless, it set her apart from all the others and let an audience know that now it was watching something special — the performance of a gifted, dedicated, and unique skater, an artist who was really going places. *A future superstar!*

CHAPTER
THIRTEEN

There was the usual reception after the performance. Becky came out of the dressing room and was immediately surrounded.

"Superb skating!"

"Magnificent performance!"

"You were wonderful, Ms. Bacall."

Someone pushed a microphone at her and asked, "How do you feel, Becky?"

"*Hungry!*" she laughed, remembering to dazzle the TV audience with her smile. What would the TV audience think, she wondered, if she gritted her teeth, scowled, and said, "Lousy!"

She didn't want to seem ungrateful, but she wished they would all leave her alone for a few minutes. She was sort of frazzled at the moment, and she didn't really much feel like making like a celebrity. Jojo Starbuck walked by, shot Becky a

smile and said, "Beautiful skating, Becky!" The
TV announcer's eyes lit up and said "*tilt.*" He
motioned to his cameraperson, and the two of
them moved off after Starbuck.

"Beanie, that flying whatchamacallit. Is it new?
I don't think I ever saw you do that before," her
father said, slipping a protective arm around her.

"Your poor father!" her mother laughed, giving Becky a kiss on the cheek. "I thought he'd
pass out he was so terrified. He's still convinced
only a contortionist can do things like that.
Lovey, I'm so proud! You were so wonderful.
The audience adored you."

"Where's Dee?" Becky's father asked, looking
around. "I want to congratulate her. She put on
some performance!"

"She's still in the dressing room, making herself beautiful," Becky replied. "She's got her eye
on Leslie Sokol. I told her he's too young for her,
but you know Dee."

Mrs. Danziger came over. She was wearing a
black dress with a plunging neckline and a big,
huge diamond around her neck. She gave Becky a
repressed peck on the cheek and said, in a re-
strained voice, "You did very nicely, dear," as
though she was paying a compliment to one of
the angels in a grade school Christmas pageant.

Vera came thundering over to drag Becky away
to meet the judges. Becky sighed, summoning up
her official, public smile. She wished she could
dispense with diplomacy for the moment. She was

108

beat. It was a strain having to meet people after a performance when she was so drained physically and emotionally. She hated having to be charming and pretend she was the all-American typical teenager. That was the image Vera wanted her to project. She could never figure out why. Why couldn't she project her *own* image? Was it so terrible? Would it turn people off? Another thing. What was a typical teenager anyway? Was there such a thing, or was it a cliché invented by an ad agency executive to sell soda, phonograph records, and acne cream?

"*Schmile!*" Vera commanded, and Becky complied.

"How do you *do*?" said the tall, baldheaded judge, beaming at her paternally. "That was quite a performance, young lady."

"Marvelous!" the second judge put in, the one with the moustache and the bumpy hair. The third judge said nothing. She just stood there looking Becky up and down with a cold, impersonal, and appraising expression. Becky felt like a racehorse on the eve of the Kentucky Derby. The third judge's name was Adrian McElroy, but people called her the "Demanding One" because she was the world's toughest judge. If you could get more than a five-five out of McElroy, everyone said you were "Super Skater."

Becky stood there smiling her wholesome, cheery, girl-next-door smile, letting Vera do the talking. Under the circumstances it was preferable. She managed to maintain control, but it wasn't easy in the crazy, hyper, post-performance mood she was in, kind of like a high but with overtones of exhaustion and depression, the big letdown. If Vera hadn't been there, standing guard, watching her like a hawk, she probably would have broken down, said something totally outrageous, and blown her cover.

"You've come a long way from Sun Valley, haven't you?" Judge Number One said.

Becky picked up on the look Vera was giving her and replied, "I was only eleven then, and I didn't have Vera for a coach either."

Vera beamed, and Judge Number One said, "Well, you've got the best coach in the business now, young lady!" Becky smiled and nodded.

"Will you be going to Lake Placid with Vera this summer?" Judge Number Two inquired.

Before Becky could reply, Vera exclaimed, "She vill!"

"Will Ms. Danziger be going too?"

"No," Vera replied with an emphatic shake of her head. "Deirdre, she iss goink to Zurich to shtudy with Anton Mueller."

Becky stood there trying to hang on to the smile, her public image dissembling. Dee going to Zurich? But that was impossible. The three of them were going to Placid together. That had been decided months ago, and Dee certainly would have told *her* if anything had changed.

"Well, keep up the good work, young lady,"

Judge Number One was saying. Becky retrieved the smile, said she would try, thanked them, and watched them walk away. She went looking for Dee, and when she found her breathlessly asked her, "How come you didn't say anything to me about Zurich?"

Dee looked up. Her eyes glazed over, the way they always did when she was about to be evasive, and she mumbled, "Oh, that. I haven't really thought about it, that's why. It's not my idea. It's Vera's. Vera's and my mother's."

"And Anton Mueller's obviously."

Dee dropped her eyes. "Yeah, well, but what's the use of even discussing it? If I don't qualify at the Nationals, I won't be going anywhere this summer, at least to skate."

"Oh, Dee, come off it," Becky exclaimed angrily. "You can con everybody else, but not me. That's all we've talked about for months, the three of us going to Placid for the summer. Even if it wasn't anything definite, you should've mentioned it to me."

Dee glanced up. Becky saw a glimmer of remorse behind the defensiveness. "Okay," Dee said with a shrug. "I purposely avoided saying anything. For one thing I knew it'd upset you because you were counting on the three of us spending the summer at Placid together. For another, well, I guess I didn't want to deal with it. I know it's an honor, being invited to study with Anton Mueller, but I don't want to go. My mother's insisting on going along to chaperone. The prospect of spending the summer in a strange place halfway around the world with *her* doesn't thrill me at all. Anyway, why would I be fainting to go to Zurich with my mother when I could be at Placid with you and Jed?" She sighed, looking woebegone. "I know it was wrong of me, not saying anything, but you know me. I figured if I ignored it, it'd go away."

"Great!" Becky said, giving her a disgusted look. Well, that was Dee all right, the "Great Pretender," the girl who coped with her problems by pretending they didn't exist. It was classic Dee Danziger behavior, and by now Becky ought to have been used to it. When they had first started being friends, it had driven her crazy. How did you deal with people like that? You never knew what was on their minds.

Over the years, mostly on account of their friendship, Dee had opened up a lot and learned to be more honest about her feelings, but once in a while, she reverted to type, regressed, and went back to being her old self, secretive and unreachable.

Dee bent to pull up her boots, looking up at Becky from under the peak of her salt-and-pepper tweed golfing cap. "I'm really sorry. I know it was awful, your finding it out that way. I should have told you myself. Are you angry at me?"

Becky gave the cap a yank, pulling it down over Dee's eyes. "Who could ever be angry at you?" she said with a smile.

Dee's face fell, and she said in a pensive tone, "My mother. She's been angry at me since the day I was born."

When Becky and her parents got home, the phone was ringing itself off the wall. They could hear it as they trudged up the front walk.

"It's probably Grandma wanting to hear all about the exhibition," her mother said, fumbling in her pocketbook for her keys.

"No, it's your sister wanting to hear all about the exhibition," Becky's father said, getting his keys out and opening the door.

"It's neither," Becky exclaimed, dashing into the family room and pouncing on the phone. "It's Jed wanting to hear all about the exhibition."

"Hey, Blades, I was just about to give up," Jed said, sounding more himself than he had the day before.

"I knew it was you," she said, grinning at her parents over the receiver.

"How did it go?"

"Great! You missed another award-winning performance by yours truly."

"I was there in spirit. Did you get my vibes?"

"I always get your vibes. Listen, you're coming

down, right? You're not going to cop out on me. We're making you a feast. Daddy says not to worry, he'll be glad to drive you to the airport Sunday."

"*Wonderful!* I was hoping I'd miss my plane."

"Don't you want to spend two glorious weeks in sunny Florida, ogling girls?" she laughed, feeling gratified.

"With my parents hovering over me, watching every move I make? No way! Besides, you know I never ogle anyone but you."

"Ask him how his cold is," Becky's father said from behind his newspaper.

"Ask him if he likes whipped cream or vanilla ice cream on his pumpkin pie," her mother called from the kitchen where she was mothering her plants.

"Daddy wants to know how your cold is coming along," Becky said.

"I told you. All I need is love," Jed replied. "Also sleep! I haven't had a night's sleep since I got here. I stay up every night studying. Yesterday I had two exams. I stayed up two nights studying, then pulled a B and a B-plus. I'm telling you, Blades, it's tough eking out a B average. Cripes, a B! I never got anything less than an A before in my life. It's very undermining. I feel like an intellectual dropout."

"Who, *you*? Don't be droll. If it's that hard for you, the boy genius, it must be impossible for everyone else."

"Becky, I don't need a con job, especially from you," Jed said in a tight voice.

"Who's giving you a con job?" she exclaimed, mildly affronted. "I'm just saying how I feel. If *you're* having trouble eking out a B, there's something radically wrong. Maybe it's too much for you, a job and school too. Maybe you're dead on your feet, walking into those exams zonked out of your mind."

She waited for his reply, absentmindedly fiddling with the books on the shelf beside the phone. Her father pretended to be intent on the crossword puzzle, but she could tell he was all ears. In the kitchen her mother had stopped crooning to her plants. "Jed?" Becky said. "Are you still there?"

"I'm here," he replied, still in that same controlled voice. "Look, I've got to go, okay? See you Saturday. The girl I'm driving down with wants to leave here real early. I should be getting to you around noon. You'll be there, won't you? I mean you won't still be at the rink . . ."

"You're driving down with a girl?" she squeaked. "Jed Hollander! And you said you were only interested in me."

"Uh, uh. What I said was I never *ogle* anyone but you. There's a big difference between ogling and interest. Don't tell me you're jealous! No, not you. It's demoralizing having a girlfriend who never gets jealous. I wish you'd work up a little jealousy, just to bolster my ego. Listen, I've got to split. I've got a class in six minutes, and the professor locks the doors so you can't get in if you're ten seconds late."

"Delightful!" she said, hanging up the phone. "That place sounds like a prison, not a school."

"So Jed's driving down with a girl, is he?" her father said, peeking at her over the top of the newspaper.

"So he tells me," she said airily, pretending not to be in the least bit perturbed by the news.

Her mother finished pinching dried leaves from her flowering begonia and carried it back to its place on the coffee table. "He could be driving down with the entire Dallas cheerleading corps, and it wouldn't matter. Jed's true blue!"

CHAPTER FOURTEEN

"I must be hallucinating!" Becky cried when she got to the rink Friday morning and Dee was already there. "You are just a figment of my over-active imagination."

"Yup! That's me. A figment," Dee replied, blinking sleepily up at her. "I was up all night, thanks to my parents. They were having another of their all-night, marathon fights. Honestly, they're like a couple of little kids, fighting over each other's toys, and Deena, Delia, and I, we're the toys. Do you know what he wants now? Joint custody. Do you believe this man? What does the father of three grown daughters, the youngest of whom is seventeen, want with joint custody? Really, I wish they'd split already and get it over with. It'd be a huge relief.

"Deena says if they do split up, my father'll

probably go back to Paris to live. He never liked it here, anyway. She says my mother'll stay, though. Deena says if he gets this joint-custody thing, that'll mean I'll have to divide up my time between them — six months with him, six with her. Frankly, I'd rather go with him altogether. He's chauvinistic, sure, but he doesn't care if I skate or not."

Becky pulled on her gloves, her mind in a turmoil. She hadn't been prepared for anything like this. Three thousand miles, that's how far it was from New York to Paris, France. Three thousand miles was a long way. You didn't pick up the phone and dial Paris, France, anytime you felt like a rap with your best friend.

Dee began her stroking, wearing just tights, a sweater, and her patriotic leg warmers that looked like American flags. Becky was bundled up to her ears and still frozen. Well, she told herself, there was no reason to panic, at least not yet. The Danzigers had been doing their routine for years, and they hadn't split up yet. Maybe they never would.

"Listen, I was thinking," she said, dropping back so Dee could catch up with her. "Even if your parents finally did split, and your father got this joint-custody thing, and he went to live in Paris, it wouldn't necessarily mean you'd have to go with him. You're seventeen, practically an adult, and you *do* have something to say in the matter. You've got a choice. It's your life, isn't it?

If you don't want to live with your mother, you could live with us. My parents would let you. I know they would."

Dee got very intent on a Mohawk, her eyes riveted on her skates. "Could I bring Cat?" she said in a tremulous voice.

Becky suddenly remembered about her father's allergies. "Oh gosh, my father's allergic to cats. But we could work something out. Maybe Deena or Delia would take Cat, just until after the Nationals. After that we'll be traveling with the team, so it'll be no problem."

"Right. No problem," Dee murmured. A single, solitary tear rolled down her cheek. One thing Dee never did was cry. Sure, she cried at movies sometimes and programs on TV. Sometimes she cried over those soppy love stories in books. But she never cried over anything that had to do with her personally. She was much too tough for that.

Becky felt helpless. What did you say to your best friend when she was hurting? In this case she couldn't console her by telling her everything was going to be all right, because it wasn't, and they both knew it.

"I hate my life!" Dee said vehemently, wiping at her eyes with the back of her hand.

"Dee, a few months from now we'll be gone," Becky said very softly. "Then it won't matter what your parents **do.** They can fight with each other twenty-four **hours** a day if they feel like it.

119

It won't be able to hurt you, because you won't be here to see it."

They got to school just as the warning bell was ringing. Becky hurried away, thinking about Paris, the battling Danzigers, Zurich, and that if the worst happened, and Dee really did have to go to Paris with her father, their friendship could be seriously affected.

"Hi, Becky. How ya doin'?" one of the boys said when she passed him in the hallway.

Sue Farber came out of the math lab, hunched over an armful of textbooks. She flashed Becky a shy smile, her braces gleaming wickedly, fell into step beside her, and said, "Anything wrong? You look like you're angry or something."

"What? No," Becky replied, smiling at her. "I just don't want to be late for homeroom, that's all."

"I guess mornings are a real hassle for you, huh?" Sue said, looking at Becky over the rims of her bifocals, her eyes filled with admiration. Becky was surprised at how really beautiful the eyes were, gray and kind of limpid.

"I wish *I* was athletic," Sue was saying. "But I'm not. The one and only time I went skating, I broke my wrist."

Becky had to stop at her locker, so she was late getting to psych. When she got there, there was a party going on. Not the usual Christmas party with decorations from the dimestore, supermarket candy and cookies and punch. Ms. Wing had stopped at the bakery and bought fresh rolls and pastries. There were cheeses from the cheese store, preserves, butter, a pot of coffee brewing, gallons of orange juice and apple cider.

After class, when she was helping with the cleaning up, Ms. Wing came over and said, "Rebecca, I've been meaning to talk to you about something. I was doing some reports in the office the other day, and I happened to glance through your file. Why didn't you tell me you'd changed your mind about college?"

Becky didn't know what to say. She was embarrassed, sure — also resentful. How come everybody was on her case all of a sudden? How come they all felt so free about sticking their noses in her private business?

"You mean you didn't know?" she said, playing for time.

"You know very well I didn't," Ms. Wing said. Becky looked up from the paper cups she was stacking. Did Ms. Wing actually look hurt, or was she imagining it? "It's criminal!" Ms. Wing said, shaking her head at her. "An intelligent girl like you. What a waste! Your parents must be very upset. I know how much your going to college means to them."

"I guess so," Becky murmured, feeling a lot like Benedict Arnold. "Ms. Wing," she went on, trying to keep her voice under control, "I'm a skater. That's what I am, first and foremost. Skating is my life, the one thing I ever really excelled at. A lot of people — people who aren't athletes — don't realize how hard it is being a skater, or at least one who's serious about skating and in competition. They don't realize how much time and hard work goes into it, the sacrifices that have to be made . . ."

"I do," Ms. Wing said very quietly. "Because I'm an athlete too, a skier. But being an athlete, that's just part of what I am, the physical part. I wouldn't dream of developing just that one part and neglecting all the others. I can't believe you're planning to."

CHAPTER
FIFTEEN

"I sure hope Vera's not going to sabotage my weekend," Becky said to Dee when they were leaving the rink after the last session that evening.

"She probably will," Dee replied, slinging her skate bag over her shoulder. "That's her idea of fun and games, sabotaging people's weekends. Wow, my feet are killing me! How come yours never hurt?"

Becky tucked her skates into her skate bag and zipped it closed. "They do, all the time. I guess I'm just used to it, that's all."

"I'm so hungry!" Dee wailed, gazing forlornly at the snack bar. "Should we have a yogurt or something?"

"You go ahead. I better not. Lately even yogurt upsets my stomach."

"No, I better skip it. There's two-hundred-and-eighty calories in one innocent-looking little yogurt. Two-hundred-and-eighty calories, and it doesn't even taste fattening!"

"Good-bye, girls. See you tomorrow. Have a nice weekend," Mrs. Williams said, smiling and waving cheerfully through the window of the ticket booth as they pushed through the turnstile. Rick was just climbing out of his new car, a nifty, electric-blue Corvette with red racing stripes. He came over and started telling them about his plans for this year's Christmas Ice Pageant. Becky fidgeted, keeping one eye on the exit door, expecting Vera to come barreling out any minute to order her to skate about sixty extra sessions over the weekend.

"Don't look now, girls. Here *she* comes," Rick muttered, making a hasty getaway. Vera came bearing down on them, looking like a WWI flying ace in a doublebreasted leather coat and combat boots.

"So! Der boyfriendt, he is cominks for the veekendt, yes?" Involuntarily she glanced over at Dee. "A little birdt, she toldt me. She saidt Vera shouldt lett you haff the veekend off, so you couldt be with him. If Vera, she letts you haff the veekendt off, vill you rest, or go out mit der boyfriendt und drink beer?"

"I don't drink beer," Becky said, sending Dee a look of gratitude. A car pulled into the parking lot. Dee piled into it, and it took off again before Becky had a chance to see who was driving.

"Dee, she hass so many boyfriendts, I loose trek of vich iss who," Vera laughed good-naturedly. "Better she shouldt haff less boyfriendts, more skatink, yes? Rebecca, I gott a phone call from John Verucci. He vants you to skate in der benefit for der Olympick fundt at Madisoane Squvare Garten next month. I toldt him you vould."

Vera was looking at her as though she thought Becky should be ecstatic. "Oh, Vera," Becky groaned, beginning to sag. "Why didn't you tell him I couldn't?" A performance, now, this soon before the Nationals, and one that was going to be on prime-time TV? And one in which every top skater in the country would be taking part? Just what she needed — like a hole in the head!

Of course she ought to feel honored. Only two or three of the best, most promising amateurs were asked, but it was difficult to feel honored when you were feeling this pressured.

"Rebecca, you *must* do it," Vera said.

"I must, I must, I must!" Becky burst out. "That's the story of my life."

"Aha," Vera said softly. "So now vee make mit der self-pity."

"No. It's not that. You know it's not. It's just that, well, I have so much work to do before the Nationals, and I've got school, and it's just so much to handle at one time, and . . ." She sighed, feeling desperate and trapped. "Well, I guess, since you already told them yes, I'll have to do it. Did Dee say she would?"

Vera shot her a quizzical look and said, "Dee, she vass not ask-edt."

"Not asked? How come? I mean, if I was, why wasn't she?"

Vera shook her head in exasperation, mumbling to herself, looking peeved and put upon. "Now Rebecca," she explained patiently, "you are no longer a child. I know how much you loff your friendt. I loff her too. Do not laff. It iss difficult not to. But you must not lett loff make you blindt. You know as vell as I do, there are many, many goot skatersz; only a few great vonz. Hardt vork, discipline, trainink, dat is how von getsz to be great. You haff vorked hardt und dedicatedt yourself. You may yett be a great skater. Dee, she iss more fun-lovink than hardt-vorkink. To be a champion, you must vant it alvaysz; vant it more than anythink in the vorld."

Becky nodded, though she didn't agree. She was just about to remind Vera about Dee's talent when a horn honked, and the Volvo pulled up to the curb. Her mother smiled and waved. Vera waved back, looking uncomfortable. She said something unintelligible, then lumbered off in the direction of the 1957 Cadillac she always parked way at the other end of the parking lot so no one could park close enough to scratch or mar it.

"I have to stop at the supermarket for a few things," her mother said when she piled into the car. "Do you think Jed would like my cranberry mold or just plain cranberries from the can?"

"The mold, I think. Anyway, I like it better."

"I wish you'd remembered to ask him whether he likes his pumpkin pie with whipped cream or ice cream." Her mother pulled into the supermarket parking lot, switched off the ignition, waited grimly while the Volvo indulged in its usual, post-operative fit, then took the key out of the ignition and dropped it in her coat pocket.

She turned to Becky with a smile and said wryly, "If we're lucky, it'll start again when we come back. What's wrong, lovey? No, don't say nothing. I know something is. It's written all over your face."

"Everything always is," Becky sighed, dropping her eyes. She wanted to tell her mother what Vera had said, but she was afraid to. Maybe her mother wouldn't react the way she wanted her to. "That Vera!" she grumbled, scowling out the window. "She makes me so mad sometimes. She's so opinionated and narrow-minded. She thinks if you're not positively fanatical about skating, you're no good. Just because Dee has other interests, and doesn't spend twenty-four hours a day at the rink, skating her brains out, she thinks she's not avid enough."

"Did Vera say that?" her mother asked. Becky nodded. Her mother sighed, shook her head, then said, in a sad voice, "Vera's only trying to prepare you for the possibility that Dee might not qualify at the Nationals. No, lovey," she went on when Becky started to protest. "Let me finish please. You're sixteen. You said it yourself. No more little girl. I know you don't like to hear me say this, but Vera is right. Dee isn't in your league. It's not that she doesn't have the basic talent. She does. It's that she's never developed the kind of self-discipline you need to go past being just an adequate skater and become a champion. You know it yourself. There's a time in every skater's career when she has a choice to make — to keep on just skating or go for broke. You made that choice a long time ago."

She reached for Becky's hand, her eyes full of love and sympathy. "Look, I know how much it means to you, how you've always planned it, the two of you going to the Olympics together. But think of the odds. Is it realistic to assume you'll both make it? Lovey, you can't plan the future. I know that better than anyone. I made plans too, so now look at me. I'm forty, frumpy, and retired. Instead of skating, I'm chauffeuring, cooking, cleaning, and sewing. Instead of a champion, I'm the mother of a champion and, believe it or not, I kind of like it that way."

She reached to wipe away a tear that had escaped and was slipping down Becky's cheek.

"Look, Vera's not infallible. She could be wrong. Dee's a stylish, talented performer. She's never done all that well with the figures, and she's not always consistent, but if she skates as well at the Nationals as she did last week at Sky, she could just pull it off."

CHAPTER
SIXTEEN

"Hi, guys, I'm home!" Becky called, taking the stairs two at a time.

"Where's she going in such a hurry?" she heard her father say to her mother.

"Becky," her mother called from the kitchen, "don't you want something to eat?"

"Later, Mom. I have to get ready."

"Ready for what?" her father said, sounding annoyed.

"You mean for whom," her mother corrected. "It's almost noon. Jed will be here any minute."

Becky stripped off her practice clothes and headed for the bathroom. She showered, shampooed her hair, blew it dry, and gave herself a quick facial using some of the gunk her mother had received as a free bonus gift for trying some beauty wizard's new product. She put on a white shirt that had once been a dress shirt of her father's way back in the old days before she was born, a tattersall vest from one of his old suits, dark gray corduroy baggies, suspenders, clogs, and a pair of knee-high, gray-and-white argyle sox.

She checked herself out in the mirror. She sure looked funky. Dee would have been proud of her, putting herself together that way without any help. She was about to head downstairs and grab some lunch when a car door slammed outside.

"Ooof!" Jed grunted when they collided on the front walk.

"Ooof yourself," she said and kissed him.

"Control yourself," he laughed. "Your next-door neighbor's watching us through his binoculars. Did you know you had a Peeping Tom living next door?"

She stepped back to get a better look at him. "Boy, you got skinny! Don't they feed you up there?"

"The food's inedible," he replied, grinning at her. "All the other guys' girlfriends send them C.A.R.E. packages." He looked her up and down, a bemused expression on his face. "Did you grow, or am I standing in a hole? It's a good thing I don't have a hangup about my height, or I'd be having an identity crisis right now."

"It's my clogs," she said, sticking out her foot so he could see. "You still have your cold," she added, ignoring her father's warnings about coming in contact with cold germs and kissing him again.

"It's been a long time between kisses," he sighed, kissing her back. "You know what? You look sensational!"

"Sorry I can't say the same about you." She was partial, but even with a cold, he looked terrific to her.

He wasn't the type most of the girls she knew would have considered handsome. He wasn't tall. He wasn't muscular. He wasn't a typical, blond surfer type, an all-American type, a sexy macho type. He wasn't any type at all. He was his own type. His face was arresting mainly because of his eyes. They were light blue and really piercing. He called them his X-ray eyes. It was hard to describe him. He didn't look like anybody else, so you couldn't make comparisons. His nose, well, it had been just an ordinary nose once. Then he'd broken it falling off his bicycle when he was in tenth grade, so now it was a nose with a lot of character. His mouth was wide and just naturally turned up at the corners, so he always looked as though he was smiling to himself. People misinterpreted that sometimes and thought he was smirking. He had terrific teeth, almost as terrific as hers. Dee was always saying that when they got married and had kids, they would be born with full sets of dazzling teeth, smiling away to beat the band to show them off.

Usually he was a great dresser. He liked funky clothes. Today he looked anything but funky in ragged blue jeans, a football jersey, Adidas, and a quilted down vest.

"The way you're looking at me, I feel like a big, juicy steak," he said, taking her arm and steering her inside. "Speaking of steaks, what's to eat? I'm starving!" He dumped his duffle bag in the guest room and followed her into the kitchen. Her mother looked up from a batch of cookies she had just taken out of the oven and smiled at him.

"Welcome home, Jedediah! My, you got thin. Don't they give you enough to eat up there?" She and Jed started discussing the perils of dormitory food while Becky made tuna fish for sandwiches. Jed ate three, plus a carton of cherry tomatoes, two sour pickles, three carrots, a whole cucumber, and almost an entire quart of milk.

After lunch they borrowed the car and went for a ride to Garnett Point. Jed wanted to take a walk on the beach for old time's sake. While they walked, he told her about school: about his classes, his professors, his job, his boss, the guys in his dorm, etc., etc., etc. She tried hard to listen and pay attention, but she was freezing to death.

"I walk around feeling so pressured all the time," he was saying.

"I kn-kn-know what you m-mean," she replied between shivers.

"My father thinks I ought to quit the job, but I feel I have to make *some* contribution. My education's costing him a fortune."

"B-but if your g-g-grades are g-g-g-going to suffer ..."

"Are you cold or something?" he asked, finally noticing her discomfort.

When they got home, her parents were both in the kitchen putting the finishing touches to the dinner. Her father was whipping cream for the pies, and her mother was basting the turkey.

"Jed, it's good to see you," Becky's father said, looking as though he really meant it. "It gets pretty dull around here without you to argue politics with."

Jed snitched a fingerful of stuffing from the turkey before her mother put it back in the oven. He gave her father a sidelong glance and said, "Mr. B, I don't mean to pry, but are you growing that thing in protest against something, or did you cut your chin?"

Becky burst out laughing. "Now will you shave it off, Daddy?"

Her father looked insulted. "Absolutely not. I think it makes me look very distinguished." He went back to his whipping.

Jed started wandering around the kitchen, sticking his fingers in the pots and pans, sampling everything, and generally getting in the way and making a pest of himself. Finally, to get him out from under their feet, her mother sat him down at the table with a bowl and a wooden spoon and instructed him to whip the pumpkin-pie filling. He went at it as though the whole meal depended on how well he whipped. Becky could hardly keep a straight face. Since when did pumpkin-pie filling need whipping?

It was a pre-Christmas Christmas dinner complete with all the fixings: turkey, corn-meal stuffing, sweet potato casserole, cranberry mold with sour cream dressing, pumpkin pie with both whipped cream and vanilla ice cream. Jed ate as though it was the first meal he'd had in months, gorging himself, having two and three helpings of everything. By the time dinner was over, and they had finished cleaning up, it was pretty late.

"We'd better get going, or we'll miss the early show," he said, taking a last lick of leftover whipped cream before putting the bowl away in the refrigerator.

"I think we missed it already," she said, giving his hand a slap.

"Well, we'll make the next one."

"But we can't. Remember I told you? Until the end of March the early session starts at seven. That means I have to get up at five, and . . ." She caught his look and added, "Hey, I'm really sorry. I didn't realize how late it was getting, or I would've said something. Look, why don't we just go for a ride or something?"

He regarded her with a solemn expression. "We already went for a ride. Besides, if you have to get up at five, you have to be in bed by nine, right? And it's almost that now. What do you suggest *I* do after you go beddie-bye? Put on my 'jammies' and watch the Late Show?"

"Don't knock it," she laughed, trying to keep it light. "I'd love to catch the Late Show sometime."

He gave her a look. "Yeah, well, after I knocked myself out getting here, the least you could do is stay up until eleven or eleven-thirty. It's not like I'm asking you to get ripped and stay out all night. Just catch a flick, maybe stop into Perry's for a beer."

He stalked into the family room, and she hurried after him. Suddenly he was in the worst mood. That just wasn't like him at all, because generally he was the farthest thing from moody. "Eleven-thirty, that means I don't get to sleep until twelve. Five hours. That's not nearly enough. After five hours you know I'm going to blow a practice session. Right now I can't afford to do that. Hey, after five hours of sleep, I might as well forget it and not go in the first place."

He gave her a look that said, *"So? Would the world end if you missed one lousy practice session?"*

"Jed, what's with you? I mean, you know better than anybody what being in training means."

"Yeah, *do* I!"

She let that one pass, thinking that too was very

136

uncharacteristic of him. "It's not just the Nationals," she went on in a placating tone. "Now I've got this Madison Square Garden benefit too, and I have to get something ready for *that*. Every practice session means a lot right now. I'm down to the wire." He was fiddling with the TV channel selector, his back to her, but she could tell just by the way he held his body that he was angry at her. "Hey," she said softly, coming to stand close beside him, "ask me anything else, and I'll do it, gladly, but I can't take a chance on messing up a practice session. Not now."

"It's sure nice to know where I stand in your life," he muttered, his back still to her. "Just after your skates and about four places down from your pro." He turned, his face tight with anger, and strode to the couch.

He reached over and took a handful of peanuts from the bowl on the coffee table, glowering at the TV set from under his brows, his blue eyes like deadly laser beams, that half-smile turning up the corners of his mouth. He began flipping the remote-control channel selector, one hand raking his hair in a characteristic gesture. "Forget it, okay? I asked you. You said no. We don't have to make a whole big deal out of it."

"What?" she asked, unable to hear him over the noise from the set.

He shot her a look. "Read my lips, Blades, okay?" Speaking with exaggerated tolerance for her obviously inferior grasp of the language, he said, *"I said it's no big deal. Did you get it that time?"*

"Did I!"

He put his sneakered feet up on the coffee table and lounged back against the pillows, flipping channels with one hand, popping peanuts into his mouth with the other. She felt like murdering him. Also like laughing. It was pretty funny, his doing the injured-lover number. The pose didn't suit him at all.

"If it's no big deal, how come you're so angry?" she said.

"Angry? Who's angry? I'm not angry. What'm I doing that makes you think I'm angry? Just sitting here, eating peanuts, watching TV, having a scintillating evening. Hey, do you believe this commercial? Those wonderful folks at the ad agency must think the American public has the collective I.Q. of fifty. Good! The *Saturday Night Movie. That's* something, anyway. Hope it's something I haven't seen." He launched into a whole satiric monologue.

She stood there wondering what to do next — yell her head off or go over and put her arms around him? Stick to her guns or give in? Chastise him or apologize? Or, in his present emotional state, go upstairs and give him a chance to simmer down?

He certainly was acting strange. He rarely got angry about anything personal, only things like politics and world affairs. He could rant and rave about American foreign policy or big business, but he never got emotional over anything personal. As her father always said, he was basically a very cerebral person. Only now he was behaving like anything but, being super-emotional, petty, and childish.

"Just sit there and enjoy your movie," she said, heading for the door. "Your towels are in the bathroom. Your bed's made. If you get an urge to raid the refrigerator, feel free." She hesitated in the doorway, expecting him to ask her not to go. "Well, good night," she offered, playing for time. She had her pride. How much could a person bend? She went out into the hallway and started up the stairs, stopping on the third one, thinking any minute he'd come flying out into the hallway and apologize.

All the way up the stairs she kept thinking he would. In her room, standing in front of the mirror, giving her hair an extra hundred strokes, listening for the sound of his footsteps on the stairs, the door half open so she'd be sure to hear. Even after she had gotten into her pajamas (and a robe in case he still came), she was still hoping. But after a half hour, when he still hadn't come, she gave it up, switched off the lights, and went to bed.

CHAPTER SEVENTEEN

It was Dee who made her see the error of her ways.

"Talk about rigid!" she exclaimed when Becky told her what had happened. "After the poor guy came all the way down here to be with you, you went to bed at nine o'clock? Oh, wow! Do you really think you'd have blown the Nationals by breaking training one night?"

"Well, no, but . . ."

"Beck, I don't blame Jed for getting angry. How's he supposed to feel anyway? He comes down to spend a weekend with his girlfriend, and she trots off to bed at nine o'clock."

"Maybe I ought to go home and apologize?"

"You bet you should! I wouldn't blame Jed if he was on his way back to Ithaca right this minute."

The thought made Becky wildly apprehensive. She hurried inside, took off her skates, got her things, and left, heading for the bus stop at the corner. Only Rick came along in his new 'Vette Stingray and gave her a lift instead, so she got home in six minutes flat.

"Where's Jed? Still sleeping?" she asked.

Her mother looked up from the cookbook she was reading, a surprised look on her face. "He went with your father to get the newspaper. What are you doing home? The session's not over 'til ten."

"I left early."

"You did? You're not sick, are you?"

"No."

"How did you get home? The bus?"

"Rick drove me. He's got a new car. It's a Stingray, blue with red pinstripes." Was she imagining it, or did her mother look piqued?

"If I hadn't had to hang around and wait until the brownies got done, I would have left here fifteen minutes ago and wound up sitting there at the rink wondering what happened to you," her mother said in a wounded tone. "You could have called. That would have been the thoughtful, considerate thing. I don't mind being your full-time chauffeur, but I do expect a little consideration. I don't like to be taken advantage of."

"Gee, Mom, I'm sorry. I tried to call, but the line was busy."

Her mother got out the potholders, reached

141

into the oven, and pulled out a batch of brownies. "I was on the phone with Dee's mother. She pretended she was calling to be neighborly, but she wanted to pump me about the Madison Square Garden thing, to find out if you'd been asked."

"What did you tell her?" Becky asked uneasily.

"The truth, of course."

"Oh, Mom! I wish you'd told her you didn't know."

"Now, lovey, how could I do that? She'd know I was lying."

"The thing is, I haven't said anything to Dee yet. I know I should have, and I keep meaning to, but every time I start to, I think of how hurt she'll be that she wasn't asked, and I just can't go through with it."

"Well, she'll be a lot more hurt if she has to find out from her mother, and angry at you for not telling her right away." Her mother chipped off a piece of brownie with her fingernail and popped it into her mouth.

Becky frowned. Her mother was right. Dee would never understand why she hadn't said something right away, especially since she was the one who was always carrying on about not hiding things from one another. Should she call Dee now, right this minute, and head Mrs. Danziger off at the pass? She wanted to, but Jed was going to come back any minute, and she had to talk to him before he left for the airport, which was soon, come to think of it. She just felt so overwhelmed. All of a sudden she had all these complicated problems. It was a lot to cope with, especially now.

"I was wondering why Jed didn't get up this morning and go to the rink with you," her mother was saying in an exaggerated casual tone.

"I told him not to bother. Why should he get up at five o'clock? He needs his rest."

"Try again, lovey," her mother said, getting out a mug and pouring herself a cup of coffee. "If I know Jed, he'd never opt for sleep if he could be with you. You two had an argument, didn't you? No, don't deny it. You were up most of the night. All that tossing and turning and pacing back and forth; that wasn't Ronald Bear."

Becky picked up the platter of sticky buns that were on the countertop and followed her mother to the table. She took a nibble from the stickier side of a bun. "Sherlock Holmes is alive and well and living in Northridge. So what's the big deal, anyway? So we had a minor disagreement. What's so world-shaking about *that*?"

"Nothing, but I don't think it was so minor. Two people don't give up sleeping over minor disagreements."

"Okay, so it wasn't all that minor. I overreacted, that's all. You know me. I'm not exactly the most adaptable person around, especially when it comes to my skating. It was all pretty dumb. Jed wanted to catch the late movie at the

Squire. I said I had to get to bed early. He thought I was being rigid, and . . ."

"Rigid? I don't call that being rigid. I call it being disciplined and diligent, what you have to be if you want to reach your goal."

"Right, but maybe, just maybe, I should've lightened up this one time and thought of him. Here he came all the way down here to be with me, and I trotted off to bed at nine o'clock and left him sitting there all alone. Dee said I should've stretched the curfew just a little bit and stayed up with him. She said she didn't blame Jed for getting mad; that if she were him she'd have been back at Cornell by now."

"Well, we all know what Dee's priorities are," her mother said, looking at her over the rim of her coffee mug. The front door opened, and Becky's father called, "Sara, I'm home. You'd better hurry. It's almost ten."

"Forget it, Alex. Your daughter left the rink in the middle of a session and came home early."

"Gosh, Mom, you say that as though it's some kind of crime," Becky mumbled.

Her father came dashing in. "She's not sick, is she?"

"No, just following your advice and taking it a little easy, Daddy, being young while I can," Becky giggled.

He mumbled something about the ingratitude of children and went into the family room to do

144

battle with the Sunday crossword puzzle. Jed came into the kitchen, looking as though he hadn't slept for a month. She felt guilty about that, too. He looked like that on account of her. He muttered something that sounded vaguely like "Good morning" and got busy pouring himself coffee. He took a few brownies, put them on a plate, carried the mug and the plate to the table and sat down next to her mother, still without even a glance in her direction. Her mother reached over, extracted a nut from one of his brownies, got up, and left the table.

"Did you sleep okay?" Becky asked Jed.

"Fine."

"How's your cold, anyway?"

"Fine."

"Want another brownie?"

"Fine."

She waited until he'd finished the brownie and another mug of coffee, then said, "Jed, let's go for a walk." He shook his head. "Please, Jed. Could we go for a walk? I want to talk to you."

He shrugged, got up, took the plate and cup to the sink, put on his down vest, and followed her outside. "Okay, what d'you want to talk about?"

"Well, that should be pretty obvious. I wasn't about to ask you for your reactions to today's headlines, or inquire how you enjoyed the movie last night."

"No?" he said coldly. She sighed. Well, he

wasn't going to be too receptive. He wasn't going to make it easy for her. Okay, she'd start with an apology and go on from there.

"Jed, I left the rink and came home early because I wanted to tell you I'm sorry about last night. I was wrong. I know it now."

He was staring intently at the tips of his Adidas, his forehead creased in a frown. "I wasn't exactly Sir Galahad myself. I shouldn't have blown my cool. That's pretty much of an ongoing thing lately, blowing my cool. I don't know what's the matter with me. I walk around feeling angry all the time, and I don't even know who or what I'm angry about."

"It's all that pressure at school," she began, moving a step closer. "People act weird sometimes when they're under pressure. Know what Dee said when I told her what happened? She said I should come straight home and apologize; that last night I was only thinking about myself; that I should've realized you were having problems and needed me to be there for you."

He spun around, eyes blazing. "You told Dee about last night? You discussed something that was personal, just between us, with her? Man, I feel like I've been had! Dee's *your* chum, not mine. I don't particularly dig her. And I don't want her sharing our intimate moments. If you can't understand how I feel, that's your problem; but I think you owe me that much, to keep what

146

goes on between us out of your rap sessions with your big-mouthed girlfriend, Dee."

With that he turned and stalked away, back to the house. She stood in the road watching him, feeling confused, hurt, and angry all at the same time. Where was all this anger coming from that he was directing at her these past two days? And why was he making *her* the scapegoat? What had she done to deserve being put in that position? She had enough hassles to contend with at the moment. She didn't need him coming down on her, too.

A car sped by, splashing her with mud. She began to follow Jed back to the house, stepping through the snowdrifts alongside the road, getting snow in her hiking boots.

She walked in the front door. He was coming out of the guest room with his duffel slung over his shoulder. He walked right past her and into the front hallway.

"You better hurry. You'll miss your plane," her mother said, coming out of the kitchen.

He opened the door. "Thanks, Mrs. B. For the dinner and everything. Guess I'll see you . . ."

"Aren't you going to say good-bye to *me*?" Becky said, heading out the door after him.

"Yeah. Good-bye!" He strode to the car, threw the duffel bag in the back seat, and climbed into the front beside her father. Her father started up the engine. It took a couple of seconds for it to catch. Jed sat there waiting. He didn't look at her. He kept his eyes straight ahead, and his mouth was set in a grim expression.

"Have a good time in Florida," she offered. "Say hi to your parents for me." She glanced at her father. He was leaning forward to look at her, a perplexed expression on his face, but for once he didn't offer any comment. He threw the Volvo into "drive." It moved forward, snorting and coughing. As it rumbled away down the street, Becky called, "Good-bye!" Jed didn't answer.

CHAPTER
EIGHTEEN

Everything was in a mess. All these problems were coming down on her at once, and at the most crucial time in her life, too. Talk about lousy timing!

It wasn't enough she had the thing with Jed to contend with. Now she had to worry about Dee too.

And, if *that* wasn't enough, there was the Madison Square Garden thing. Dee's mother must have said something to her about it by now. How was Becky going to explain to Dee why she had never said anything? She was in a quandary. She was finding out it was next to impossible to be a true and loyal friend and an honest one, too.

"If I tell her, she'll want to know why I didn't say anything before," she said to her mother when they were driving to the rink next morning.

149

"Why didn't you?" her mother asked.

"You know why! Because I didn't want her to be hurt. The reason she wasn't asked is they didn't think she was good enough."

"Lovey, that's not your problem. And Dee's not your responsibility. You aren't doing her a favor protecting her from the truth. Life's full of disappointments. She'll have to take hers, just like the rest of us."

"But don't you see, Mom, they're wrong!" Becky protested. "She *is* good enough. They're just being unfair."

Her mother pulled up at the rink entrance. Becky waited, but she didn't say anything else on the subject. Becky knew she wouldn't either. She might be dying to, but she'd control herself because she believed Becky had to figure this one out for herself.

Becky went inside. All the time she was getting ready, she debated with herself. When the session started, and she went out on to the ice, she still hadn't made up her mind.

Dee showed up about ten minutes after the session started. She came skating out, straight over to Becky, looking as though she was ready to take on the entire Northridge boys' hockey team.

"Well? Are you going to do it? Are you going to let that tyrant Vera intimidate you into doing that Madison Square Garden thing?"

"Uh, *what*?" Becky had a fleeting image of the

scene that must have taken place between Dee and her mother. It was *her* fault Dee had had to find out this way. If she had said something right away, it wouldn't have happened.

"You aren't going to do it, are you?" Dee persisted. "Because that would be dumb!"

Becky muttered something about dumb being pretty much of a characteristic trait in her case. Dee shook her head, looking exasperated. "You aren't overextended enough? The word 'no' isn't in your vocabulary?"

"Well, it's just that . . ."

"Vera knew better than to ask me. She knew I wouldn't do it!"

"Oh, but . . . Yeah, I guess so." Becky stole a look at Dee's face, but Dee wasn't covering up, pretending or being evasive. She really meant what she had just said. Becky hated herself for feeling relieved that now she wouldn't have to explain why she hadn't mentioned the benefit in the first place. Dee skated off. Becky got back to work, feeling even worse than before. A few minutes later she looked up and saw Dee leaving the ice.

"Where are you going?" she called after her.

"My sister's picking me up. We're going into the city to a rock concert. It's Christmastime, remember? The jolly holiday season, with a ho, ho, ho? I, for one, do not intend to spend the whole vacation in a damp, cold skating rink, skating my brains out. That is because I, unlike someone else I could mention, am a real, live person, not a robot on skates."

"You mean that's it for today? You're not skating again?" Becky was dazzled by Dee's audacity. If Vera showed up, and she probably would sometime during the day, Dee would really be in trouble. She thought of taking a break, then decided not to. She had a lot of work to do, even more now because of the benefit. She was doing something very different from her usual thing, something kind of flashy and very contemporary to a Barbra Streisand song. Vera, the strict classicist, disapproved, but Becky wasn't going to let that stop her. She wanted the Olympic Committee to see she was a versatile skater and not locked into one style.

She worked some more, then gave in and took a break. Let's face it, even *she* couldn't be "Super Skater" when she was feeling this low. Dee was wrong about her being a skating robot. She had emotions just like everyone else, and lately they were messing up her head!

Christmas. Who cared? It was hard to feel merry when you had so much on your mind. She wished she could take a real vacation. It would be so great to spend a couple of weeks on a beach somewhere, nothing to do but lie in the sun, swim, snorkel, catch up on her sleep. She had a bikini she hadn't even worn yet, a white one that really would have shown off a tan. Jed flipped for blondes with suntans in white bikinis.

She thought of him, basking in the Florida sunshine, probably surrounded by girls. The way he had left — no kiss, no hug, not even a good-bye. It didn't exactly make her feel like the most loved, cherished girl around.

Maybe he would call her. Or she could call him. She would wait. If he hadn't called by the weekend, she'd put through a person-to-person call to his hotel in Miami. Or maybe she shouldn't wait. Maybe she should call him right away, to-night.

Becky finished her ice cream and went back outside. Just knowing she was going to do some-thing decisive made her feel a lot better. She went back to work, but it was hard to concentrate. She kept rehearsing things she would say to Jed.

"You got mail," her mother called down from the upstairs landing when she got home. Becky checked out the manila envelope lying on the table in the hallway. Inside were two college cata-logs, one from Hofstra, one from C. W. Post. At-tached to the latter with a paper clip was a scribbled note from Ms. Wing:

"It occurred to me you might like to have a look at these. Have you thought of going to a local college instead of an out-of-town one? Of perhaps taking just a few courses to begin with, ones you could work in around your skating schedule? That way you could get started on your college education without overburdening yourself. Let's talk about this and see what we can work out. Have a happy holiday."

Camilla Wing

She'd heard about teachers taking an interest in their students, but this was ridiculous!

"Ms. Wing's really on my case," she said to her mother. "She's not just fooling around."

"Who is?" her mother replied from inside the linen closet where she was folding the clean towels. "No one who cares about you is happy about your decision, but it *is* your decision. You're the one who'll have to make it."

"Funny, the way everyone's been acting, I thought it was theirs," Becky said, heading for her room. She flopped down on her bed and began to leaf through the catalogs. The psychology courses sounded fascinating, especially the advanced ones. Before you were allowed to take those, you had to have a year of introductory psych. It sounded like a pretty long haul. At that rate, how long would it take for a person to become a full-fledged, licensed, and practicing psychologist? Twenty years?

"Anything interesting?" her mother said, trying to sound casual.

"I guess, if you find course descriptions in college catalogs interesting. One thing, anyway. Ms. Wing's right. I could work out a schedule around my skating if I wanted to."

"Well? Do you want to?"

"I don't know. I thought this was one decision I had already made, one thing I didn't have to think about anymore. You know how with the skating you can never plan anything in advance. If you win a competition, you go on to the next. You don't know where you'll be going next until you know the outcome of a competition. There's always that tension, waiting to see what happens. It was a relief knowing that this was one thing that wasn't pending. I had decided, and that was that."

"Well, as I said, it's your decision," her mother said, reaching to straighten the needlepoint picture of the figure skater over the dressing table. "Of course it isn't something you can't change your mind about. You aren't making an irreversible commitment. If you decide to go to college, there's no law that says you can't change it again if it's too much for you, and you feel you can't handle it. Everthing in life doesn't have to be as binding as your commitment to your skating."

"No, I guess it doesn't," Becky said, getting up and starting from the room.

"Where are you going?" her mother asked.

"To make a phone call," Becky replied. "I want to see if Ms. Wing's at home."

CHAPTER NINETEEN

She tried to reach Jed that night. There was no answer. She was disappointed, especially after she had worked herself up to making the call in the first place. She decided to try again the following night.

She got home from the rink the next day an hour early, thanks to Vera who had an appointment with her dentist. When she walked in, there it was, a letter from Jed, addressed to her, Ms. R. V. Bacall, in his familiar chicken-scratch scrawl.

"You got a letter from Jed," her mother called from the kitchen.

"I know."

"How about some rice pudding? I just made it. It's good for your stomach."

"In a minute, Mom. Something I've got to do first." She picked up the letter and went upstairs.

Alone in her room with the door closed she turned it over, reading and rereading the return address: *Shelbourne Hotel, Miami Beach, Fla. 33140.* She could just imagine the Shelbourne Hotel, a pink stucco place on the beach with lots of girls in it. She had a pretty good idea what was in the letter. Once she had read it, it wouldn't be just a pretty good idea anymore. Of course she *could* be wrong. It could be one of his usual letters, a newsy one about his vacation, a satire on life among the wealthy in decadent Miami Beach.

She ripped open the envelope and spread the letter out on her knees.

"Dear Becky," it began, a dead giveaway at the outset. Jed would never start a letter "Dear" anyone. He always said that if the envelope had your name and address on it, you could be fairly sure it was meant for you.

"Well, one weekend, and everything is changed. I feel like a heel, but in a way I'm glad I finally got some of the things I've been feeling out. It's a bummer, though, when all along you've been deluding yourself you're Sherlock Holmes, and you find out you're Professor Moriarity instead.

"I've been doing a lot of thinking down here, about us, mostly, and about what a crummy year I've been having. I guess I'm pretty messed up. My father keeps telling me that being messed up is normal at my age, but that's just like him, isn't it, refusing to acknowledge that the apple of the collective family eye might have a worm in it?

"I love you, but I can't go on indefinitely sharing you with your pro, your skating schedule, the U.S.F.S.A., and all your other priorities. Your skating doesn't leave enough for me. I need someone who'll be there for me a hundred percent, who'll put me first, not second. Right now I can't cope with being number two, even for you.

"There's this girl up at school. She's not a girlfriend-type girl, just a friend-type girl, a girl you can really rap with. Lately she's helped me through a few bad times. I told her all about you, and she said it must be wonderful to be so talented and have everything going for you. She says she hasn't got any special talents, other than being a good listener. I guess she's right. She's just 'Plain Elaine, the Listener.'

"Well, I'd better close. I'd wish you luck, but you don't need luck. When you're rich and famous, I'll be telling everyone I know, 'See that super-looking girl with the long, blonde hair and the sensational smile? She was once my girl.' "

The letter was signed simply, "Jed."

Becky put the letter away in her desk. She went to the window. In the driveway behind their house the next-door neighbors' kids were playing Star Wars. She glanced at the photograph of Jed she had taken at the beach the summer before. That had been the best day! Driving home later Jed had whispered to her, "I love you, Blades. Without you I'd be the loneliest guy in the world."

She began to cry. She was surprised, because she hadn't felt it coming. Not that she was the most stoical person around, but she wasn't a crier, either. Only when she finally *did* cry, she *cried*. Not just a few, stray tears. A real deluge, Niagara Falls.

What was it her mother was always saying? Nothing like a good cry to make you feel better. Well, she didn't know about anyone else, but crying didn't make *her* feel better at all. It made her feel worse.

That was the end of that. A relationship that had weathered twelve long years, over in minutes, terminated by a two-page letter. Was Jed already thinking of her as "his old girlfriend," the one he had outgrown? Was he already going out with someone else, some flirty suntanned girl in a white bikini?

"He certainly has perfect timing," her mother said when Becky showed her the letter. "Right before the Nationals. Why didn't he just come down here and run you over with his motorcycle and break both your legs?"

Becky's father kept saying Jed would be back;

159

that a person like Jed didn't end a twelve-year relationship just like that, with a "Dear John" letter, unless he was under a lot of pressure and not responsible for his actions.

"As soon as he gets his head straightened out, you'll hear from him," he kept saying.

"He's right," Dee agreed when Becky told her what her father had said. "As soon as he's thought things through, he'll realize how crazy this whole thing is."

Becky didn't know. She wasn't sure of anything anymore. She had thought she knew Jed inside out; that she could pretty well predict what he would do and not do. It just went to prove how wrong about a person you could be, even one you had known all your life. You could think you knew a person inside out, then find out you didn't know him at all.

She threw herself into the skating, grateful to have an escape. She put a lot of time and effort into preparing the piece for the Madison Square Garden benefit. As it turned out, she needn't have bothered. She never got to skate it, anyway.

She was all dressed and ready, putting the finishing touches to her hair, when the stomach cramps hit her. One minute she was fine. The next she was lying on the floor, doubled up in agony. Her parents put in an emergency call to Doctor Arlen. Five minutes later he was walking in the door. He didn't even want to examine her;

160

he just took a hypodermic needle out of his medical bag, filled it, and gave her a shot. Almost before the needle was out of her arm, the pain was starting to subside. *Then* he examined her.

"What's wrong with me, Doctor Arlen? What've I got?"

"Are you sure you want to know? You're not going to like it."

She felt a quick stab of apprehension. She began conjuring up all sorts of grisly things, like maybe dying at an early age of some dreadful disease. She imagined the movie that would be made about her, posthumously of course, the most promising Olympic hopeful in years, struck down in her prime just on the brink of superstardom.

"The condition can be arrested," Doctor Arlen said, looking as though he didn't really think it would.

Condition? Arrested? It sounded terminal. Maybe it wasn't fatal, though. Maybe she'd just spend the rest of her life chained to a wheelchair, a hopeless cripple.

He dropped his stethoscope back in his medical bag. "What you've got is a case of extreme nervous exhaustion, the result of pushing yourself too hard."

"Pushing myself too hard? That's your diagnosis?" she chortled, mentally pushing the wheelchair off the nearest cliff. "Is that the name of a real disease, 'Pushing Oneself Too Hard'? Is it in the *Medical Encyclopedia* or the *Physicians'*

Desk Reference? What do I look it up under? 'P' for Pushing? Imagine how it will look on an absence excuse. 'Dear Ms. Parker, please excuse Becky's absence. She's been suffering from a severe attack of "Pushing Herself Too Hard." ' "

"Very amusing," he grumbled, giving her an all-suffering look, "but if you aren't careful, 'P' for 'Pushing Yourself Too Hard' could turn into 'U' for Ulcer."

Her parents reacted on cue, both of them at once. Becky tried to be calm. An ulcer. But that was a grownups' disease. It came from being uptight, having too many worries, too much responsibility, too little fun.

"My uncle has an ulcer. He takes these little pills."

"Yes, well, you're going to have to do a lot more than just take pills," Doctor Arlen said. "You're going to have to be on a very rigid diet, watch every single thing you eat, get more rest, learn to relax more, cut down on the skating . . ."

Her parents were holding their breath, waiting for her to respond. "Doctor Arlen, I'll do whatever you say, except for one thing. I won't cut down on the skating."

"But . . ." her father began. Her mother shushed him with a look, came over, and sat down on the bed. "Lovey, remember when you were sick, what we said about your stopping the minute it got to be too much for you?"

"Mom, *we* didn't say that. *You* did. This is my

162

decision. No one else can make it for me, even you."

It wasn't that she didn't understand what Doctor Arlen was saying, or that she didn't recognize the risks, or that the idea of getting an ulcer didn't terrify her. It was just that the idea of not skating in the Olympics terrified her even more. When the chips were down, it was a no contest. Even something a whole lot worse than an ulcer wouldn't stop her now.

"Mom, I can't cut down on the skating, especially not now. I'm going to skate in the Olympics next year, even if it means skating in them with an ulcer!"

Her mother didn't say a word, just sat there looking at Becky as if to say, *"Well, I taught you to be independent. Now I'll have to live with it."* Her father was standing with his back to them. She could tell by the way he held himself how upset he was.

Doctor Arlen was looking down at her, a curious mixture of concern and admiration in his eyes. For a few minutes no one said anything. Then he sighed, shook his head, and said, "My, what a determined young lady!"

She shot him a grateful smile. "If I weren't, would I be skating in the National Championships two weeks from today?"

CHAPTER
TWENTY

Dee was in one of her funny moods. Becky recognized all the signs. It usually happened right after a school vacation, when they had to go back to the same, old, boring routine. Skating and school. School and skating.

They were on their way to the rink. When they got to the top of Vista Hill, Dee backed up, took a running start, then slid all the way down, almost landing in the snow piled up at the bottom. She started cavorting around, pretending to be freaking out, waving her arms and yelling.

"I'm sick, do you hear me? Sick, sick, sick! I hate skates. I hate skating. I hate *ice*."

Becky caught up with her at the bottom of the hill. "Brr, it's cold! But cold or not, I have to work out."

She got to the rink and into her skates, and hurried on to the ice. It was a lot colder inside than out, a nippy ten above. She started stroking, trying to get warm. A boy came out and started to skate around in front of her, hockey style, his hands clasped behind his back, his body hunched over his skates close to the ice. He was wearing a quilted down vest just like Jed's.

All of a sudden everything reminded her of him. The shampoo, for instance. The balsam-scented shampoo at home in her bathroom. *He* used that brand. The same brand of toothpaste, too. There were dozens of other things, too, every-day things: certain songs, things people said, places in town where they had been together, even the oversized football jersey he had given her she sometimes wore to bed.

She pushed the thoughts away, forcing herself to concentrate on work. She was working on the short program for the Nationals, getting the sequence of movements fixed in her head. There were three parts to the National Championships, skated on three subsequent days: the compulsory figures, the short program, and the freeskating. The short program was the part most skaters dreaded. All the movements were prescribed in sequence by the U.S.F.S.A. You had to follow them to the letter. Also, you had to skate those movements within a two-minute time limit. If you goofed on a jump or a spin, you didn't get to do it over. One chance. That was it. That's why the short program was the ultimate test of a skater's skill and control.

Becky's mother had just finished her costume, a dress of sheerest chiffon the color of a summer-evening sky with tiny silver sequins sewn all over it that looked like twinkling stars. It had an uneven hemline and was draped over one shoulder, leaving the other shoulder bare. Her father said it looked like a Greek toga.

One thing she was sure of. No one could be better prepared than she. When she stepped out on to the ice at that coliseum in Cincinnati, she was going to be the best-prepared, most practiced, most confident skater alive!

She was working out the final sequence of movements, getting the timing just right, when Dee came out and started stroking around the rink, making like a Dorothy Hamill special on TV. Suddenly she felt it, a subtle change in the atmosphere, something in the air that hadn't been there a moment before. The hockey skater shot past her. Dee whizzed by. Becky looked up. Standing at the barrier watching her was Jed.

She was startled, yes, but not all that surprised. She had thought she might be seeing him before too long. She began to skate toward him, her mind racing. Well, now that he was here, how should she react? Should she be cool and aloof? Semi-receptive? Downright hostile? Should she talk first, or let him? And, if the former, what should she say?

She tried to read his expression. Those cool, laser-beam blue eyes were watching her warily. What had he come for? What was there left to say after that notorious letter? Or had he changed his mind?

The thought made her angry. What did he think she was, a yo-yo? One minute he wanted her. The next, he didn't. Did he really think he could change his mind like that, and she would go along with it?

She arrived at the barrier. He didn't say a word. She made a futile stab at levity: "Well! How's 'Elaine the Listener'? Still listening?"

"Could we talk?" he muttered. "I think we ought to talk."

"*Talk?*" she echoed, sounding exactly like a parrot. "Oh, sure. Talk! Wait here. I'll get my things."

The Volvo was parked at the entrance, the motor still running. She got in, reached under the dash, and flipped on the heater. Freezing-cold air began to pour from the vents.

"I forgot. It's broken," she said, shivering involuntarily.

"If I put my arm around you, will you scream?"

"Why don't you try it and see?"

Cautiously he slipped an arm around her shoulders. She thought he'd try and kiss her and was disgusted with herself for being disappointed when he didn't. He looked awful, and that made her feel good. Good for him if he'd suffered. He deserved to suffer. Hadn't he made her suffer, too? Still, his eyes looked so empty and so sad. She made herself remember how cold and angry they had looked the last time she had seen him, and that strengthened her resolve.

"Well?" she began, giving him a challenging look.

"Well," he began. Then he sighed. It was a world-weary sigh that came from deep down inside him. "I had it all rehearsed and memorized, a whole, long, eloquent speech. About how wrong I've been, how sorry I am, how much I've missed you. But frankly, this has been the worst week of my life. I'm just too shook emotionally to do a decent job of it. No, don't look at me like that. I'm not trying to enlist your sympathy. Just telling it like it is. The truth is I don't have the heart for soaring eloquence at the moment, so I hope you'll accept a simple, heartfelt apology, spoken in a few, brief words . . ."

She burst out laughing. "Jed Hollander, you never said anything simple, or in a few words, in your life! The nerve of you, sitting here talking about how miserable you've been and how shook up you are. What about *me*? What about what you did to me? You're so selfish and self-centered, you never even gave *me* a thought!"

She stole a look at his face. "You're right," he

said in a pathetic-sounding voice. "I am selfish and self-centered. The most selfish, self-centered guy in the world!"

"Well," she began, feeling she had to defend him, "you *have* been under an awful lot of pressure . . ."

"I acted like a rat, and I know it. I wouldn't blame you if you never forgave me."

"Oh, but I understood!" she protested, putting a hand on his arm. "I wasn't angry. Not at all. After we had that fight, I thought about it and realized you were right; that I was being rigid and selfish. I came to you the next day, ready and willing to apologize, but then you said those things about Dee, and . . ."

He shot her a guilty look. "I didn't mean what I said. I only said it to hurt you. You know how I feel about Dee. Well, you ought to after all this time. If I didn't like her, wouldn't you have known it long before this?"

"Yes, if you were being straight with me."

"Being *straight* with you? When have I been anything else? Isn't that what our whole relationship is all about, being straight with one another? The only time I wasn't being straight was when I wrote that dumb letter. I don't even know why I wrote it. I must have been flipping out. The minute I mailed it, I was sorry. If I could have gotten it back, believe me, I would have."

"You would?"

"Of course! Don't you think I knew what reading that letter would do to you? Especially now, when you've got so much on your mind already. That's why I left Florida early and came here. I had to tell you that I didn't mean what I said; that I love you and need you; that I'd rather have you, with your crazy schedule, your curfew, your compulsion to skate, than anyone else in the world!"

She threw her arms around him, and they sat there holding on to one another for a while. Finally she said, "Now that I think about it, that letter didn't sound like you at all. If you told me someone else wrote it for you, I wouldn't be surprised."

"Talk about split personalities," he said, and smiled. "I feel like a real *schiz*! I've been doing a lot of crazy things lately, you know it? And I've been finding out a lot of things about myself, too. I always thought I was strong, an emotional powerhouse, the kind of person who had his feelings totally under control. But now I realize that wasn't the real me at all. Underneath I'm not strong. I'm weak. It's sort of a shock, when you've always thought of yourself as a strong person, finding out you're a weak person instead."

"Weak? Who says you're weak? Just because you found out you're human and can have problems like everyone else, doesn't mean you're weak. Who do you know who goes through life without problems?"

"My father! At least that's what he wants everyone to think. He's always trying to make me into a he-man like he is, mostly to impress other people. He wants people to say, 'Luke Hollander's kid? Yeah, that's some fantastic boy! That boy's really got it all together.' That's my public image, 'Kid Fantastic.' Even *I* believed in it. Only, down deep inside, where it really counted, I wasn't 'Kid Fantastic' at all. I was 'Kid Nothing.'"

"Who, you? Don't be dumb! So you found out you're not perfect. So, okay. But that doesn't mean you're a nothing. Look, I'm sort of relieved. It would be intimidating having a boyfriend who was perfect, especially since *I'm* so imperfect."

"Your parents are ready to kill me," Jed said when they were on their way home. "I feel like a rat, letting them down like that. They've always been so great to me."

"Don't worry," she assured him. "They too know it's okay to be imperfect." Knowing her parents, her father would probably be the difficult one. Her mother, well, she was more understanding.

When they got home, it was just the other way around. Her father was the one who was semi-agreeable; her mother, super-difficult. Her mother could hardly bring herself to say "hello." All during dinner she kept sending Jed these hostile looks, as though she'd like to kill him. Becky was glad when dinner was over. She cajoled her father into agreeing to drive Jed to the airport, but, when she expressed her intention to go along, her mother put her foot down.

"It's eight-thirty. You're going to bed. Remember what Marshall Arlen said."

"What'd she mean by *that*?" Jed asked when he and Becky were alone, saying good-bye.

"Oh, nothing. Just that I've been getting these stomachaches, and Doctor Arlen's convinced that, if I'm not extra-careful, it could turn into an ulcer. But you know *him*, a real old lady. You get a little indigestion, and he wants to check you into the nearest hospital."

"An ulcer? Gee, that's serious. You don't fool around with an ulcer."

"Who's fooling around? I'm not fooling around. And besides, it's not an ulcer. And it won't turn into one. Right after the Nationals I'm going to take a rest. Then that'll be the end of my stomachaches."

Jed put his arms around her, kissed her, and said, "It just better be! I don't want the girl I love walking around with ulcers."

That night she lay in bed thinking. It had been a painful experience, but something good had come out of it, too. For one thing they had gotten some of their feelings out into the open and learned more about one another. From now on Jed wouldn't have to go around being "Super Kid." He could relax and be himself. And she wouldn't have to feel she had to live up to a boyfriend who was perfect.

CHAPTER TWENTY-ONE

The day before they were supposed to leave for Cincinnati it snowed.

"It's a bad omen," Dee said when she called Becky early that morning to say good-bye.

"Baloney! Snow's lucky," Becky replied. "I wish you weren't leaving today. I wish we were flying out together tomorrow like we planned. It'd be so much more fun."

"You know my mother," Dee said. "Heaven forbid she shouldn't spend the most money of anyone. I don't know why she wants to go out there a day early and spend all that time hanging around the hotel doing nothing unless it's *that*. She wants to have the record for the most money ever to be spent on an Olympic contender in the history of the civilized world!"

The snow continued all day and into the evening. Becky was up practically the whole night, watching out the window, worrying herself over whether or not they'd make it out of their driveway, no less all the way to the airport, and whether, if they did, the plane would be able to take off with all that snow on the ground.

"Well, this is it. We're actually going," her father said, stowing the last of their luggage in the trunk of the car next morning.

"Did you call the airport?" Becky asked, marching around in the snow on the front lawn to see how deep it was.

"I did. The planes are leaving on schedule."

"I can't believe we're actually going," her mother said, climbing into the front seat. "After eight, long years."

"Has it really been that long?" her father mused. "It seems just yesterday you took her skating for the first time, Sara. Those little skates with the red pompoms, remember? And that little red skating skirt you made her? Wasn't she beautiful?"

"Beautiful? I was a fat *klutz*!" Becky smiled, remembering that first time. She had been so proud. Plenty of the other kids' mothers skated, but hers didn't just skate, she *skated*, like one of the stars of the Ice Capades. The kids had been so impressed. They had treated her like some kind of celebrity after that.

They got to the airport an hour early, her father's punctuality phobia at work again. When you went anywhere with him you always spent a whole lot of time waiting around.

"I wish Dee was flying out with us," Becky said, checking out the paperbacks on the revolving rack at the bookstall. "It's just so typical of Mrs. Danziger to make a great big deal about flying out early. She always has to be the one to be different."

"Oh, I don't know," her mother replied, eyeing the chocolate bars on the candy counter. "Why not, if they can afford it? I wouldn't mind having that extra day."

The plane ride was a real ego trip. Some of the flight attendants knew who she was, and they kept coming over to talk to her and bring her goodies. The other passengers noticed all the attention she was getting, and a rumor went around the cabin that she was a starlet under contract to a big motion picture studio.

Cincinnati was digging out from under a snowstorm, too. The airport was a disaster zone. It took them an hour to find a taxi to take them to the hotel. When they walked into the lobby, the first person Becky saw was Dee. She came flying over, in a state of nervous collapse.

"I've been *frantic*! I thought something must've happened to your plane. You're so late. My mother's been nagging at me to go upstairs and go to bed, but I couldn't. Not until I knew you were okay."

Becky's mother suggested they all have a

snack. The coffee shop was full of skaters. Becky recognized most of them. A young man in a leather coat came in, and she whispered to Dee, "Isn't that Charles Tickner? It *is*! Everybody says he's a cinch to win the men's."

Dee gave her a poke. "*Psst!* There's Linda Fratianne. No, not that one. The one over there with the dark hair and the red coat. And there's Tai Babilonia! Gosh, she's beautiful! And she wears the most gorgeous clothes."

They went on celebrity-watching while they finished their milk and sandwiches. As they were walking out of the coffee shop, Becky said, "I sure hope Jed gets here early tomorrow morning, before the bus comes to take us to the practice rink."

"What?" Dee squealed, grabbing her arm. "Jed's coming? Jed Hollander, lately extinct boyfriend, recently revived, is coming *here*?"

"Shhh! Everybody's looking at us," Becky whispered, disengaging her arm. "Yes, he's coming. I couldn't believe it either when he called to tell me. Would you believe my parents knew all along, but they never said one word?"

"It's almost eleven," her mother said, taking her arm and starting to steer her toward the elevator. "You girls have got to get to bed."

"I wish we were sharing a room," Becky called back over her shoulder.

"So do I!"

"That's just what you both need," Becky's

mother snapped, propelling her into the elevator and pushing the "up" button. "To sit up all night gossiping on the eve of the National Championships."

Becky was up at a quarter to five, fifteen minutes before the alarm was due to go off. Like a computer, she was programmed for a quarter to five A.M. She'd probably have to get up at that exact time every morning for the rest of her life, whether she liked it or not.

Jed arrived while they were in the coffee shop having breakfast. He came in looking sharp in a leather jacket, brown corduroy baggies, a bottle-green turtleneck sweater, and a beige tweed golfing cap.

"Who's the hunk?" Becky heard one of the girls at the next table whisper. Jed sat down and leaned over to give Becky a kiss, and the girl grumbled, "Darn! I was hoping he was unattached."

Jed ordered breakfast. While he was waiting, he proceeded to devour most of Becky's, which was actually okay with her because she was too nervous to eat, anyway. He was particularly charming to Dee, asking her all about her love life and how she was doing.

They were practicing at a place called Cincinnati Gardens. Jed said it sounded more like a beer hall than a skating rink. As he was finishing the last of his scrambled eggs, Vera came in to tell them the bus had arrived. He was going to go with them, but at the last minute he decided not to, explaining that he'd probably be better off catching up on his sleep.

The practice session went okay, except that the atmosphere at the rink threw her a little. Everyone was so grim, so turned in on themselves and singlemindedly uncommunicative and unfriendly. She kept catching the other girls looking daggers at her when they thought she wasn't looking.

"If looks could kill, I'd be dead," she said to Dee.

"If you weren't my best friend, I'd probably be looking at you like that, too," Dee replied. "You're the competition, the one to watch out for after Fratianne and Allen. What do you expect them to do, love you?"

After the session they went upstairs for the official draw ceremony, kind of a dignified grab bag to determine the skaters' positions in the programs. There was a big box with folded-up pieces of paper inside. Dee was the first one to draw. She drew a second, a second, and a third.

"What a bummer!" she groaned, looking dejected.

"Just be glad you didn't draw first in anything," Becky told her. "Poor Allison Saunders drew first, first, and sixth."

When it was Becky's turn, she closed her eyes and sent a silent prayer to the deity who protected all figure skaters: *"Please, great ice goddess, give me a break!"* She wound up drawing third in the compulsories, fourth in the short program, and fifth in the freeskating, which was pretty coincidental really, three consecutive numbers.

That night after dinner she and Jed went for a walk. It wasn't exactly walking weather, but she felt so hyper, so anxiety-ridden and keyed up, she just had to get out and work some of the tension off.

"Can't you turn your brain off temporarily?" Jed complained, panting from the exertion of keeping up with her. "You're freaking me out."

"I'm skating in the Nationals tomorrow, and *you're* freaking out," she mumbled, slowing her pace. "Do you realize that the next three days will decide the rest of my life? Do you have any idea what this whole thing means to me? Can you understand that, if I don't make it, I will *die*?"

He gave her an incredulous look. "You really mean that, don't you?"

"Sure I do!"

"Blades, think about it objectively, if you can. It'll be a big disappointment, sure, but not skating in the Olympics isn't something you die from. What if you qualified and decided you didn't *want* to skate in the Olympics."

"What? No one would be crazy enough to decide a thing like that!"

"Why? What if there were something you'd

rather do, something that took precedence over the skating. Not everyone's as committed or singleminded as you. There *are* other things a person might consider just as important: going to college, dedicating your life to the theater, medicine, research, another career."

"Jed, I don't know about *other* people. I just know about me. And for me skating is it!"

"Okay, let's try another approach," he said dryly. "Is not skating in the Olympics a tragedy comparable to some others you can think of? Contracting a fatal disease? Going blind? Getting crippled in an accident? Losing someone you love?"

"Gosh, I never thought of it *that* way." She suddenly realized what he was saying. He sure had a way of putting things in perspective. She did have a tendency to lose sight of things sometimes, to get carried away. She ought to realize how lucky she was, how much she had going for her, other than the skating.

Her positive attitude lasted until she was in bed that night, lying in the darkness trying not to think. Then the scaries started up again right on schedule, zapping her when her defenses were down and she was vulnerable. Okay, so not skating in the Olympics wasn't like dying at an early age from some terrible disease, losing someone you loved, getting crippled, or going blind. But it *was* what she had built her whole life on and made all those sacrifices for. She had everything at stake, and the thing was if she didn't make it, where did she go from there?

She started to imagine how she'd feel if a year from now instead of skating at Placid, she was home in Northridge watching the winter Olympics on TV. She was beginning to lose her cool when the door opened, and her mother stuck her head in.

"Still awake? What's the matter, lovey? Too excited to sleep?"

"Too terrified, you mean."

Her mother came and sat down beside her. "That isn't going to help any, being terrified."

"Mom, I know I shouldn't feel this way, that it's wrong, but I can't help it. If I don't make it, I'll just *die!*"

"No, you won't," her mother said, taking her hand. "Whether you make it or not, you'll still have a lot to live for. You'll still be you, a beautiful, intelligent, wonderful girl on the brink of a rich, full life."

"Oh, Mom! You sound like one of those ads for the Armed Forces. '*Join the Army and live a rich, full, and rewarding life!*' "

"Do I? I do, don't I? Well, what I mean is, you'll have a lot of other options. You could go into a show. Travel. See the world. From what I hear, that's what Dee's going to do if she doesn't qualify."

"Who told you that? Mrs. Danziger? Sure, she's got Dee's whole life planned. One of these days she's going to get a surprise. Dee has plans of her own. No one can plan her life for her, least of all her mother! Mom? Dee keeps saying that, no matter what happens, or which one of us wins, things'll always be the same between us. But I keep thinking if one of us makes it, and the other doesn't, things'll have to change, won't they?"

Her mother nodded. "I think they would anyway, don't you? Now that high school is over, you two will be going off to lead your separate lives. You won't be spending anywhere near as much time together. Your relationship won't be as constant or intense. You'll be meeting new people, making new friends, developing new interests."

Becky sighed. "That's what I'm afraid of. Mom, don't you sometimes wish things wouldn't change? That they'd stay the way they are forever?"

"Yes, I do," her mother said, looking sad. "I guess every mother does. But *you* mustn't feel that way. Not at sixteen with your whole life ahead of you." She leaned forward to kiss Becky on the cheek and tuck the blankets around her. "Try and get some sleep. Other problems will have to be put aside for the time being. You have tomorrow to think about, and that has to come first."

CHAPTER TWENTY-TWO

Next morning was gray and cloudy. It looked as though another storm was brewing. Climbing out of the cab that had taken them to the Coliseum, Becky shivered inside her quilted down parka.

"There are the Danzigers," she said as a big black Caddie pulled up alongside, and Mrs. Danziger stepped out, resplendent in a new mink coat.

"It certainly is the right weather for mink," Becky's mother said, a hint of envy in her voice. Becky grinned. Knowing Mrs. Danziger, she would have worn the coat even if the temperature had soared to ninety.

Dee came over, looking pale and tired. "I didn't sleep one minute the entire night," she complained, grabbing Becky's arm and starting to pull her away.

Becky threw Jed and her parents a helpless look. "I feel like a lamb being led to slaughter. Daddy, don't look at me like that. It was just a joke. My mother's having an identity crisis, I think," she said to Dee on the way down the corridor. "She's reliving the time she was competing."

"My mother's not reliving anything. She's just living my life," Dee muttered. "If she says another word about how I ought to skate the figures, or tells me to smile or act happy, I'll give *her* the skates and tell *her* to go out there and do it."

Vera was waiting for them outside the dressing room, pacing back and forth, muttering to herself, the infamous mouton coat thrown over her shoulders, making her look even more like a Prussian general than usual.

"If one of us doesn't make it, she'll be opening that Hungarian restaurant sooner than she thinks," Dee said.

Becky fished in the pocket of her parka for her stomach pills. She wanted to make sure to take one now, before she forgot. Her stomach was feeling kind of queasy, and her throat was so dry she could barely swallow. She looked around the room, wondering if the other girls were as nervous. Fratianne glanced up from lacing her skates

185

and smiled at her. She smiled back, a little self-conscious and shy in the presence of a real celebrity. Over in the corner Allison was sitting on a bench with her head in her hands. Becky wondered if she was crying.

"Come on!" Dee said in an impatient tone, glaring at her in the mirror. "Get over here and put on your makeup. It's getting late."

Becky obeyed, wishing Dee would cool it. She had already put her makeup on. All she had to do was some finishing touches. It took her two seconds, and she wound up waiting for Dee. They were the last ones to leave the dressing room. As they ran down the corridor, Becky could feel Dee's hand, ice cold and trembling, in her own.

"Did you take your pill?" Vera asked when they got to the arena.

"Yes, I took it." The arena was packed. Becky had never seen so many people in one place at one time. *"Don't clutch,"* she told herself. *"They're just people."* Her parents and Jed came in. Her parents were smiling. The smiles looked strained, as though they had been pasted on. Jed handed her a rose. Handing out roses, that wasn't his style.

"Last time you gave me flowers was in day camp when we were picking buttercups," she said.

Mr. and Mrs. Danziger and Dee's sisters arrived. Mrs. Danziger was talking to a tall, skinny guy in horn-rimmed glasses, telling him how difficult it was being the mother of a figure skater, what a continuous strain she was under, how demanding her role was.

"He's a reporter," Dee whispered to Becky. "He was going to do a story on *me*, but by the time she gets through with him he'll be doing one on her instead."

The executive director of the U.S.F.S.A. came out to make the usual announcements. Becky closed her eyes, dropped her head forward, and began to massage the muscles at the back of her neck. Her mother came to stand beside her.

"You okay, lovey?"

"Sure, I'm okay. Are you okay, Mom?"

"No, but I'm not the one who's skating, so it's okay if I'm not okay."

"How about Daddy? Is he okay?"

"Yes, he's okay, after a fashion."

"Well, isn't it nice everyone's so okay?" Jed muttered, eyeing the executive director, who was still out in the center of the rink, talking his head off. "Is this guy always so long-winded?"

The first skater skated out, Allison Saunders, the chubby darling, wearing hot pink trimmed in rosebuds and a wreath of rosebuds in her hair.

"Is she skating or getting married?" Dee sneered. Throughout Allison's performance Dee did her whole hysterical routine, acting as though she was going to have a complete emotional breakdown any minute.

"She's really a wreck. Is she going to be able to skate?" Jed asked.

When her name was called, Dee stepped out on to the ice and underwent the usual metamorphosis, from nervous hysteric to cool, calm, and serene professional. Jed was speechless.

"That's some great parlor trick!"

"Yeah. Wish I knew how she does it."

"Never mind. Let *her* do the parlor tricks. You just skate!" Becky's father said.

Dee sailed through the figures. Considering how much she hated doing figures, and how she avoided doing them whenever possible, it was miraculous. She racked up twenty-eight points and skated off, triumphant.

Becky gave her a hug. "I'm so *proud* of you!"

"It was nothing, really," Dee grinned, acting bored. "Now shut up and breathe, Bacall. The air quality in here ain't all that terrific, but it's all we've got, so go! Well, Mother," she said, turning to Mrs. Danziger, "aren't you going to tell me what I did wrong?"

Mrs. Danziger didn't respond. Dee's sister Deena put her arms around Dee and said, "I've never seen you skate better. You were terrif!"

Becky started her breathing. When she heard her name over the loudspeaker, she stepped out on to the ice. Everything was going to be all right. She was where she was supposed to be, doing what she was supposed to be doing, and doing it the only way she knew how. Nothing could possibly go wrong.

She sailed through the figures, but then, she had expected to. Nobody put more time and hard work in on figures than she. As Vera was always reminding her, it paid off.

"I can't believe how great we were," she whispered to Dee when they were back in the dressing room. "Do you realize that between us we just racked up fifty-nine points?"

"We're terrific!" Dee said, really up, on an all-time high, feeling the elation that comes after a top performance. Fratianne walked in, followed by Lisa-Marie Allen and Allison Saunders.

"Sensational skating, you two," Fratianne said.

"Ditto," Dee replied airily. Outside in the corridor she squealed, "Can you imagine Fratianne complimenting *us*?"

Everyone went to bed early that night. Becky was exhausted, but she didn't sleep all that well. She kept waking up, thinking that it was morning and she had overslept. When it finally *was* morning she could hardly get out of bed, she was so tired.

"She's running on nervous energy," she heard her mother say to her father when they were going downstairs for breakfast. "She's only slept a few hours since we arrived."

"Have you looked outside?" Dee said when Becky sat down beside her at the table in the coffee shop. "There's a blizzard going on. We'll never get to the Coliseum in this weather."

"We won't?" Becky squeaked, beginning to panic.

"That's what you call a positive attitude," Jed said, giving Dee a look.

"Well, how do you propose we get there?" Dee replied, returning it with interest.

"Maybe we should all go together," Becky suggested. "Maybe it'd be safer."

"How do you figure that?" said her father. "If we get stuck, no one will get there."

One of the pros had driven to Cincinnati from Minnesota in his jeep, and he offered to make as many trips as it took to get them all to the Coliseum in time.

"Thank goodness we made it," Becky sighed, following Dee into the dressing room. "Imagine if they'd had to call off the National Championships on account of the weather."

She got out her lip gloss and started putting it on. Dee took a hair pick from her makeup case and began to fluff out her hair. Suddenly Becky was reminded of another scene in front of the mirror in another dressing room, the one at Northridge Rink just before the annual Christmas Pageant when she and Dee were eight and nine respectively.

It had been their debut. Rose Red and Rose White, two gawky little girls in homemade costumes. Well, hers had been. Dee's mother had

had hers made by a dressmaker. Baggy tights, rhinestone tiaras, paper wands with Christmas stars attached. You waved them and magic happened, Dee said. Becky had fallen during the performance and cut her leg. She still had the scar as a memento.

"Remember Rose Red and Rose White, the 'Christmas Klutz Sisters'?" she said, smiling at Dee in the mirror.

"Who could forget?" Dee laughed. "My mother still has that costume packed away in moth balls in the attic. She's saving it for her granddaughter. We sure go back a long way, don't we?"

"We sure do! And we'll be going *on* a long way together, too."

"You really think so?"

"You better believe I do!"

Dee smiled. Becky wasn't sure whether it was a happy smile or a sad one. As they hurried down the corridor she said, "Well, even if we don't, we'll *still* always be friends."

The program was late getting started, thanks to one of the judges who had gotten stuck in a snow-drift outside of town.

"Why did it have to snow? Why can't things ever go smoothly? Why does it always have to be so hard?" Becky wailed.

"You can't control the weather," Jed said, giving her a look. "Just be glad we got here. We could've gotten stuck at the hotel, you know.

Look, if you're uptight, breathe. It'll calm you down."

The program finally began, almost a half hour late. Allison Saunders skated out and took her position. Her music began, and she pushed off, heading for the first jump, skating as though her life depended on how fast she could get the piece over with. She was skating sloppily, out of control. Becky could tell she knew what was happening but couldn't do anything to stop it. She felt sorry for her, but there was something Allison Saunders had going for her that she and Dee did not, and that was her age. She was only fourteen. If she didn't make it to the Olympics this year, she still had the next year and maybe the next.

Allison raced through her piece, skated off, and burst into tears. Becky watched, horrified. If it could happen to Allison, could it happen to her, too?

"What's the matter?" her mother asked when she saw the stricken look on her face.

"Nothing. She's projecting, that's all," Jed murmured. "Blades, that can't happen to you, and you know it. You're much too good, too controlled. Look, stop thinking. Just lean on me, go limp, and *breathe*!"

"I'll try." She closed her eyes and tried to ignore Allison's sobbing. Jed was right. It couldn't happen to her. Not her, the skating robot, the mechanized skating machine with the built-in, electronic timer and the bionic blades. And besides, she wasn't a fourteen-year-old beginner. She was sixteen, an experienced skater. She had already gone through the sectionals and the regionals. She was practically a pro.

"I'm okay now," she said, opening her eyes. Dee's name was called over the loudspeaker. Dee skated out, looking like a beautiful princess in a pale-blue chiffon dress with a low neckline and loose, flowing sleeves, and a garland of braided blue satin ribbons wound through her hair. She was skating to a Jacques Brel song. Her music began, and she moved forward, heading for the first jump, skating a little more conservatively than usual. But that was all right. Even the most professional, accomplished skaters tended to hold back and take less chances at a crucial time like this. She moved through the first jumps, began the turning moves preparatory to the axel, and lifted off. Suddenly the timer in Becky's head sounded a warning. Was Dee falling behind?

The axel was slightly off. Not much. Just enough for her to lose a few seconds. It seemed to throw her and affect her confidence. She went into the salchow thirty seconds behind schedule. As she cleared the ice, her foot shot out from under her, and she fell.

There was a gasp from the audience. Mrs. Danziger muttered, "Get up!" But Dee *was* up, picking up her program at the precise instant she left off, hardly a beat in her rhythm missed.

"What a pro!" someone said.

She went into the upright, the sit spin, the lay back, all a little on the late side, losing precious seconds with each.

"I blew it!" she muttered, coming off the ice, the smile still frozen on her face. The girls skated out with the scorecards: two fives, two four-eights, a four-seven.

"Tough luck!" someone said. Dee spun around and stalked out of the arena.

"Where's she going?" Allison Saunders said. "What a poor sport!"

Becky stood there staring after Dee, not knowing what to do. Should she go after her? Bring her back? Should she try to comfort her, or leave her be?

"Stop all that emoting and breathe!" Jed commanded.

Linda Fratianne was skating out, a five-foot, ninety-eight-pound powerhouse in a red dress. Becky experienced a moment of stark terror. This was the girl she was competing against, the girl who was considered one of the top women skaters in the world.

"I said *breathe*!" Jed whispered in her ear. She closed her eyes, willing herself to block out the image of the girl in the red dress and substitute an empty canvas, a blank, white movie screen, a freshly whitewashed wall.

She filled her lungs with air, held it to the count of sixty, exhaled, inhaled again. Her hands and feet began to tingle warmly. She could feel the fresh supply of oxygen coursing into her bloodstream, building her energy, restoring her confidence, erasing her anxiety. This was it, her moment, the one she had been working toward practically her whole life, and she wasn't going to let it get away from her. Not for anything or anybody. Jed was right. She had to think about herself now. Nobody else. Selfish or not, that was the way it had to be. Success, that was the name of the game, at least the way *she* played it.

CHAPTER
TWENTY-THREE

"Ms. Rebecca Bacall from Northridge, Long Island."

"Chinz up, shouldersz back, und schmile!" Becky could almost hear Vera saying.

Her music began. She glided forward, moving into the first jump, fear and anxiety gone now, her entire concentration focused on what she had to do, knowing instinctively the timing she had to achieve at the very outset for the piece to work out right, down to the last millisecond. A series of connecting steps moving in a diagonal across the rink, the camel with a change of landing foot, the axel. She could sense how well she was doing, and the knowledge gave her added confidence, making her feel invincible. The timer in her head ticked steadily away, reckoning seconds. *"You're doing okay. That's my girl!"* she thought. She was exactly where she was supposed to be, halfway through her program with sixty seconds behind her and sixty left to go.

The two-jump combination was next: the double, then the triple. The flying sit spin, the upright, the lay back spin with two foot changes. She slowed, came out of the spin, arms above her head and one leg behind the other, knee slightly bent. A curtsey. Another. She skated off, acknowledging the applause with a little bow, and stooped to gather the flowers strewn over the ice, bowing again. Anyone watching her would have thought she was the coolest, most poised and professional skater in the world.

She stepped off the ice, her mind in confusion. She felt disoriented and so strange. Everything was spinning around. People standing right next to her looked as though they were yards away. Their voices sounded hollow and tinny.

"Is she okay?" somebody said.

"She's fine!" Jed gathered her in his arms. She buried her face in the folds of his jacket. "Hang on," he whispered. "I've got you. Everything's going to be okay."

"What's the score?" her mother said. Becky turned and saw the girls skate out with the scorecards. Two five-nines, a five-eight, another five-nine, and *a six*.

"A six!" Allison Saunders exclaimed, envy in her tone.

Fratianne whispered, "She earned it!"

There was a whole lot of excitement going on all around her, but Becky wasn't aware of it. She kept seeing that scorecard, the one with the big six on it.

"I did it," she murmured, letting her head fall forward on to Jed's shoulder. "I really did it!"

The dressing room was hot and stuffy. Becky felt as though she were suffocating. She got her things and escaped. The corridor was jammed with people. They crowded in on her, congratulating her, asking her questions.

"How about a couple of quick pictures, Ms. Bacall?"

"I'm sorry. I'm not feeling very well . . ."

"Just a couple of quick ones, Ms. Bacall."

Becky was about to comply. Jed appeared, grabbed her arm, and pulled her through the crowd. "She said *no*," he snapped, giving the photographer a nasty look.

As they started down the corridor, the crowd came after them. Then someone said, "Look! There's Fratianne," and in a moment she and Jed had been abandoned, and the crowd was closing in on Fratianne instead.

Her parents and Vera were outside, ensconced in a taxi, waiting to take her back to the hotel. She collapsed in the back seat beside her mother, closed her eyes, and rested her head on the padded seat back. The window was halfway open, and the fresh air felt good. Okay, two down, and only one more to go. One more day, and it would all be over. If she could just hang on one more day . . .

The thing was not to think. Just to let herself go with it. If she thought too much, she would get upset, and if she got upset, well, she might blow it. She just had to be strong and hang on for one more day.

They were planning on going out for dinner to a Chinese restaurant near the hotel. But at the last minute Becky said she couldn't, that she was just too tired. Her mother called room service and had dinner sent up. Becky managed to eat most of it. Then she took a hot bath and got into bed. By a quarter to seven she was asleep.

She awoke feeling a lot better, less apprehensive and uptight. It was amazing how a good night's sleep could straighten out your head sometimes.

They did the freeskating in front of a packed house that afternoon. She wasn't as nervous as she had been for the compulsories and the short program. The piece went beautifully, even the new jump spin. She earned another six and four five-nines and a two-minute standing ovation. As she skated off, she heard someone say, "Well, that's it. It's Fratianne, Allen, and Bacall."

Fratianne, Allen, and Bacall. It had a nice ring to it. Of course Bacall, Fratianne, and Allen would have sounded even better, but she had never expected to take a first, not at sixteen, a relative newcomer, competing against seasoned skaters like Fratianne and Allen.

Even though she didn't score all that high, Dee was the *real* star of the freeskating. There was a whole lot of public sentiment for her. People were saying she was a fabulous skater who had gotten unlucky, but who deserved to win. Becky watched her fly across the ice, skating just the opposite of conservatively now, really letting herself go, putting everything she had into her performance. It was as if she knew this was her final one and wanted to give the audience something to remember her by. She finished the piece and started to skate off. Then, almost as a parting gesture at the end of a brief but brilliant career, she did the same thing she had done at Sky the day of the exhibition — skated over to the bleachers strategically in front of the judges, dimpled up, and blew a kiss. The audience went wild.

"That girl's really got it," Becky heard someone say. "She's got star quality."

After the program was the awards ceremony. The executive director came out to announce the three winners, the young women who had taken first, second, and third place, and who would be going to next year's Olympics as members of the U.S. figure skating team. Becky stood in the entryway, holding on to Jed's hand. She knew it had to be Fratianne, Allen, and Bacall. They were the three who had scored highest. Still, what if something went wrong? What if there was some kind of a mixup? What if the judges stopped the ceremony to announce that they had given her someone else's score by mistake?

"What's *she* so nervous about?" she heard Allison Saunders whisper. "She already knows she's won."

Becky heard her name and stepped forward, her legs shaking. She could feel the perspiration dripping down her back under her dress. She could feel all those eyes glued on her as she skated out to the center of the rink and climbed up on to the platform beside Fratianne. The executive director congratulated her and hung a medal around her neck. Everyone applauded. Fratianne kissed her, and a slew of photographers rushed forward and started taking pictures, nearly blinding them with their flashbulbs. Becky was numb. Why didn't she feel anything?

She came off the ice, looking around for Jed and her parents. Dee came toward her, arms outstretched.

"Congratulations!" she said and hugged her. "What's the matter? I thought you'd be flipping out. You made it. Aren't you ecstatic?"

"I guess I'm in shock."

"You sure looked good up there! Like you really belonged. All that hard work finally paid off, didn't it? Listen, I've got to go. My mother's having conniptions. But I'll see you back at the hotel, okay? Come up to my room and we'll rap."

It took them ages to get past all the reporters and photographers and well-wishers.

"Why don't you lie down?" her mother said when they got back to the hotel.

"Later, Mom. I want to see Dee."

She took the elevator to twelve and knocked on Dee's door.

"Who is it?"

"*Me*. Who else?"

Dee opened the door. "I thought maybe it was Scotty Hamilton. He said he might drop by."

"Really? Scotty Hamilton? Dee, are you putting me on?"

Dee laughed. "Of course I'm kidding, you dumbhead. What would Scotty Hamilton want with *me*? Here. Sit down. I ordered some pizza. It's pepperoni. See, I'm having my own private orgy. I figure after the last three days, I deserve it."

"What're you wearing to the party?" Becky asked, watching Dee attack a piece of pizza.

"Nothing. I'm not going." Dee saw the look on her face and added, "Look, it's a winners' party. Not for losers. To the victor belongs the spoils, and all that jazz. Besides, I'm too beat. All I want to do tonight is sleep."

Becky nodded. So it was happening, the thing she never thought would. They were acting like two people who were mere acquaintances, not intimate friends — uptight and self-conscious with one another.

"Dee, I know it'd be easier for you not to, but please go. For me."

Dee helped herself to another slice of pizza. "Listen, this is grownup time. You can't bring your security blanket, your Teddy bear, and your best friend to the Olympics with you. Besides, you don't need me. You've got your parents and Jed, Vera, all your adoring fans. . . ."

Becky laughed to cover her agony. "Dee, please . . ."

Dee put down the pizza. "Now look, I want you to go and have a ball. This is your big night. Go and enjoy it. And stop trying to be Joan of Arc. Beck, are you going to cry? Come on, Beck, you're not going to *cry*, are you? Oh, this is dumb! Beck, *stop crying!*"

"I can't help it," Becky snuffled, wiping at her eyes with the back of her hand. "I feel so . . . so *guilty!*"

"*Guilty?* Because you *won?* That's what you were supposed to do, dopey. What should you have done? Lost to keep me company? Listen, just because you did the normal, natural thing, that doesn't make you a bad friend." She grabbed a handful of tissues from the box on the night-table, came and sat on the arm of Becky's chair. "With you for a friend, a person doesn't need any-one else . . . ever! Wipe your nose. And stop crying. You'll make your eyes all red and puffy. Sure you don't want some pizza?"

"No. No, thanks. I'm not hungry."

"You don't know what you're missing. Twelve-hundred calories in every slice and worth every bit of it. Oh, I almost forgot to tell you. Some guy called me up before and asked if I would audition for John Curry."

"*What?*" Becky flew out of her chair. "*This* you almost forgot? *This* you almost didn't tell me? A chance to audition for John Curry? *The* John Curry, star of *Ice Dancing*? Dee, for gosh sakes, do you realize what an honor that is? He was here. I saw him. He saw you skate, so naturally he wants you for his show. I can't believe it. John Curry! One thing your mother is right about. You really *do* have star quality. And John Curry recognized it right away. Watch out, Jojo Starbuck. You're about to be replaced. Here comes the *new* star of *Ice Dancing*, the beautiful, sophisticated Deirdre Marie Lisette Danziger!"

"Hey, take it easy," Dee said, looking amused. "Even if he did make me an offer, it wouldn't be for a starring part, just something in the chorus. Anyway, even if it *was* a starring part, I'm not sure I'd want it."

"Not want it? Dee, are you crazy?"

Dee flicked at an imaginary speck of lint on her trousers. She took an emery board from the nighttable and began to file her plum-lacquered nails. "What it is is a question of priorities. I'm thinking ahead. Ten years from now, when I'm pushing thirty, which do I want to be, an over-the-hill figure skater or a fashion designer with bread?"

"Dee, what are you talking about? What do you mean, thinking ahead? How many people do you think get a chance like this? Dee, a chance like this comes once in a lifetime. You'd have to be crazy to pass it up."

"Then I'm crazy," Dee said, putting down the emery board, looking up at Becky. "Beck, I've had it with skating. I'm sick to death of the whole thing. You know I've never felt about it the way you do. I like it sometimes, sure, but other times it's a great big drag. I'm ready to move on to other things. If I'd qualified, it'd be one thing. But I promised myself that if I didn't, I'd quit, pack it in and start developing some of my other talents. I want to *do* things, *see* things, earn lots of money. Like I once told you, I don't want to wind up someday just an *ex*-figure skater. You understand, don't you?"

"Sure. I understand." Becky thought of what her mother had said, about their lives going in separate directions. Was it happening already? Were they already drifting apart?

"I wanted you to know how I feel," Dee said, watching her with a thoughtful expression.

"I understand. Like you said, you never wanted it anywhere near as badly as I did anyway."

205

"That's right." Dee came over, slipped an arm through hers. "It's getting late. You'd better go. If you need any help with your hair or your makeup or anything, just call. I'll come running."

"You always do," Becky said, and left.

CHAPTER
TWENTY-FOUR

Alone in her room, getting ready for the party, Becky thought about what Dee had said. Was Dee covering up, or did she really mean it? Becky couldn't tell.

In the mood she was in it was hard to feel like partying. This was the party they should have been going to together, making the grand entrance they had always planned, walking in arm-in-arm, the "Dynamic Duo," *the winners*.

She finished making up her face and got into her outfit: purple satin jeans, a matching silk shirt, a vest in purple, teal, and cerise stripes. She headed down the hall, the disco pouch her mother had made her slung over her shoulder, her hair crimped, parted in the middle, and fastened at the sides with two flowered combs.

"Good evening," she said when Jed opened the door. "I'm Rebecca Bacall from the Greater Cincinnati Escort Service. I've come to escort you to the ball. You look *gorgeous*!" she exclaimed, checking out the midnight-blue velvet jacket, pintucked, white silk shirt, and gray flannel trousers. "Where'd you get the jacket? Is it new?"

"Uh, uh." He did a pirouette for her inspection. "I borrowed it from a guy in my dorm. And speaking of gorgeous, whatever happened to that skinny kid from Northridge with the braids and the Levis?"

Her parents came out of the elevator, her father wearing a suit *and* a tie, her mother in a black silk jacket and matching trousers.

The party was in full swing when they got there. Everyone who was anyone was there—all the skaters, their pros, relatives, friends, and a slew of instantly-recognizable, and very well-togged, celebrities. When they walked in, there was a flurry of applause. Nothing all that world-shaking, but more than Becky had been expecting. After all, who was *she* compared to Frati-anne, Allen, Tickner, and Santee?

A waiter in a fancy tuxedo showed them to their table. "If only Dee were here," Becky said to Jed. "She really digs all this cornball stuff."

"You mean she's not coming?"

"That's what she said, but she could still show up. You know *her*. She can never resist a party, or a chance to get dressed up and make an entrance, fashionably late, of course."

"Of course!"

A photographer advanced on them, flashbulbs popping. She scowled up at him. He went on snapping pictures a mile a minute.

"Would you *mind*?" she said. "It's very hard to have a conversation when someone's popping flashbulbs in your face."

"Stop scowling," Jed whispered, giving her a nudge with his elbow. "Here comes the E.D."

The executive director of the U.S.F.S.A. was bearing down on them, smiling his official, public smile. Without a word he took her arm, pulled her to her feet, and propelled her across the dance floor and up on to the dais.

Becky stood there wondering what to do with her hands. "Ladies and gentlemen," the executive director bellowed into the microphone. "May I have your attention, please?" Everyone turned around. Becky tried to smile, but her face felt paralyzed. Was he going to ask her to make a speech? "Ladies and gentlemen, I give you the youngest member of the U.S. Olympic figure skating team, Rebecca Victoria Bacall!"

Becky gulped. Everyone started applauding. Photographers were rushing around taking pictures, blinding her with their flashbulbs. The director pumped her hand. She croaked, "Thank you! Thank you very much!" and fled the dais. When she got back to the table, her parents were being interviewed by a famous TV talk-show hostess.

"Tell me, Mr. Bacall," she said, addressing Becky's father, looking over his head directly into the TV camera, "were you always a hundred percent for the skating?"

Becky's father turned, smiled into the camera like an old pro, and said, in a voice oozing with charm, "No, as a matter of fact, I wasn't, but I was always a hundred percent for Beanie."

"Beanie?"

"Beanie. That's my daughter's nickname. I gave it to her when she was little. About three or four, as I remember. She *loved* lima beans. They were her favorite food."

Becky grinned. Her father was a natural to replace Johnny Carson on late-night TV. She could see he was really enjoying himself and would have gone on reminiscing for the TV camera indefinitely had the talk-show hostess not yanked the microphone out from under his nose and shoved it under her mother's instead.

"Tell me, Mrs. Bacall, you were a figure skater yourself once, weren't you? Do you ever skate anymore?"

"No," Becky's mother replied, glaring at her. "*She* skates. I'm the chauffeur."

"Mom, you scared her off," Becky said when the poor woman had gone away. "I wonder why she didn't want to interview you," she said to

Jed. " 'Tell me, Mr. Hollander, how does it feel to be the boyfriend of a famous celebrity?' "

"Hungry!" Jed said, making a grab for the bread basket.

"She could still show up," Becky said, eyeing the doorway. "It's still only nine o'clock. Bet she'll come strolling in any minute, looking bored, wearing something totally outrageous." Her parents looked at one another, the kind of look that meant they knew something and were contemplating whether they should divulge it or keep it under wraps. "Okay, guys? What do you know that I don't?"

"How could we know something you don't," her father said, "when you know everything?"

"Alex, I think we ought to tell her," Becky's mother said. Becky tensed, waiting for the other shoe to drop. "Dee's gone," her mother went on, watching for her reaction. "They left about an hour ago. I think Mrs. Danziger must have decided suddenly, because they were in a big rush."

Becky didn't say anything. "You shouldn't have told her," her father said to her mother. "You've ruined her evening."

"No, she hasn't, Daddy." Becky picked up her spoon and started in on her fruit cup. "It's nothing so world-shaking. I just thought she might change her mind. For my sake."

"Isn't that asking an awful lot?" Jed said. "I mean, think of how you'd feel if you were in

211

Dee's position. It's not too terrific attending a victory party when you're not a victor."

Her mother shook her head. "I have a feeling she would have come. If it had been up to her, I mean. If her mother hadn't dragged her away."

"Do you really think so?" Becky said, brightening.

"Well, don't you? You know Dee. She said she wasn't coming, but I have a sneaking suspicion she intended to . . . for you."

The party lasted until after midnight. By that time Becky had gotten her second wind. She felt she could have stayed up all night dancing.

"You're still the world's best dancer," she said to Jed when they were up in her room later.

"This is true," he replied, taking off the borrowed jacket and laying it carefully across a chair. He sat down on the couch. "Alone at last! Quick, before there's a knock on the door, and it turns out to be an emissary from Merv Griffin. Come on over here, and let's neck."

"Okay, but wait until I get out of this outfit and into something more, uh, comfortable."

"You know, there's such a thing as *too* comfortable," he said when she came back, wearing Levis and a football jersey. She sat down. He put his arm around her. "It's good to have you all to myself for a change. From here on that won't happen too often. I'll have to get used to sharing you with the whole Olympic figure skating team, the reporters, the photographers, Vera, your hair-dresser, your dressmaker, your business manager, your . . ."

"Hey, I'm skating in the Olympics, not going to Hollywood. Me, plain old Becky Bacall, skating in the Olympics! Can you *believe* it?"

"Of course I can believe it. And there's nothing even remotely plain about you. You know, you really scared me the other night, the crazy way you were talking. I was afraid if you didn't make it, you'd do something nutty."

"I might have. I don't know. I don't care what anyone says. After you spend eight years of your life working toward a thing, have your parents knock themselves out making it possible for you, sacrifice friends, a social life, nearly cancel out a college career, and almost lose a top boyfriend in the bargain, it would be pretty tragic if you wound up a loser. I don't love myself all that much for saying this, and I probably wouldn't say it to anyone but you, but as bad as I feel about Dee, and as much as I counted on both of us making it, if one of us was going to win, I'm sure glad it was me!"

CHAPTER
TWENTY-FIVE

Jed's plane left first thing in the morning. Becky and her parents weren't leaving until late that afternoon. Everyone else had checked out of the hotel, and it was kind of depressing sitting around the lobby with no one to talk to and nothing to do, especially after all the excitement of the past three days.

The plane ride home wasn't exactly the up of the century, either. They ran into some turbulence outside Philadelphia. Practically everybody got sick. If the flight attendants recognized her, they didn't show it. They were too busy running up and down the aisles with paper bags.

It was really a letdown. Not that she had been expecting brass bands, but after taking a third in the National Championships, people usually got a little more attention than *this*!

The airport was a whole different story. There was a whole bunch of reporters and photographers waiting to descend on them when they got off the plane. Becky couldn't figure out how they knew anyone important would even be on that plane, unless they had spies in Cincinnati, or why so many of them would go out of their way to come to interview and photograph *her*. After all, she wasn't a Hollywood movie star, a rock singer, a visiting dignitary from the Far East; she was just a figure skater who'd come in third at a national competition.

"Better get used to it," her father said when she expressed her surprise, glaring at a photographer who was trying to climb over him in order to get a closeup. "You're a celebrity now."

"The Olympic Committee's public relations department will be promoting you," her mother put in, laughing at the way Becky was hamming it up for the photographer. "They'll want you to project a nice, bouncy, bubbly, ingenue image. Hah! I wish them luck. If Vera couldn't do it, no one can."

A reporter pushed his way through the crowd and asked, "How does it feel to be a winner, Ms. Bacall?"

"Very un-private!"

Her mother burst out laughing. "And this is the girl who used to fall apart every time she saw a TV camera!"

"She's rising to the occasion," Becky's father

said, taking both their arms and steering them through the crowd, looking authoritative and rather menacing. They spent fifteen minutes collecting their luggage, then made a mad dash for the parking lot. "Now if the car will just start," he said, unlocking the door.

"You'll *have* to get a new car now," Becky's mother murmured, climbing in. "How will it look, a big celebrity driving around in an old heap like this?"

"She's no old heap," Becky protested. "She's an original. She has style and personality. She's unique!"

"She may have style and personality," her father sighed, fitting the key into the ignition, "but I think, at this point, I'd cheerfully trade style and personality for dependability."

For once in its life the Volvo started up right away, purring like a kitten as it turned out of the parking lot. Becky snuggled down under the car blanket, grinning to herself. "I'm not much of a world traveler, I guess," her mother was saying to her father. "Every time I go away, I can't wait to get back. I wonder how my plants are. I hope they're okay. Did you know plants can feel rejected, just like people do?"

"They'd better get used to it," Becky's father said. "From here on you're going to be a world traveler whether you like it or not. Come to think of it, *I'd* better, too. If I thought I was lonely when you and Beanie were doing the regional junket, imagine how I'll feel when you two are off touring the world!"

"Alex, it won't be Beanie and *me*. It'll be *Beanie*. She's a big girl now. She doesn't need her mommy tagging along. She'll be going off with the team, and I'll be staying home with you."

Her father didn't look all that thrilled about that particular piece of news, but he knew better than to say anything. Becky felt a pang of apprehension.

She hadn't thought about it before, but of course that was the way it would be. She would be on her own. In a lot of ways, that was good, how it should be. But it was scary, too. Because it meant change, and change, well, that was something she had never particularly excelled at. She wasn't exactly the most relaxed, adaptable, or easygoing person around.

Well, the Nationals were behind her. The World Championships, coming up. Then there would be the summer, Lake Placid, training with Vera, and spending her free time with Dee and Jed. . . .

How naturally the thought had evolved. She thought about the summer, and automatically she pictured it with Dee and Jed. Only Dee wouldn't be there. Dee wouldn't be in a lot of places Becky had always planned and expected her to be.

She wondered. A year from now, if they ran into one another, what would they have to say? Would they still have anything in common, or would they have grown apart? People changed, didn't they? Especially in a year. And this was going to be one heck of a year! *She* was probably going to do a whole lot of changing.

She thought of the overworked, overtired girl who worked out every morning in front of the mirror, whispering *"That's my girl"* to herself. But that was the *old* Becky Bacall. The *new* Becky, well, she would be different. No more shying away from cameras. No more projecting phony images. No more doubting herself and getting all uptight. She was a winner now. She was good. She had proved it. Now she was going to be confident. Now she was going to be herself!

Take it or leave it. This was the real Becky Bacall. Accept no imitations or carbon copies!

"Did you hear that, Johnny Carson? Are you listening, Time magazine? This is the real Becky Bacall, bionic skater, future gold medal winner, national champion, and girl superstar. Watch out, Fratianne, Hamill, and Starbuck. Move over, and make room for me. If I can get my thumb out of my mouth and keep my knees from knocking, I'm on my way. I'm going to be the biggest, brightest superstar of them all!"

The Volvo pulled into the driveway. Becky climbed out and went around back to help her father unload the luggage. "Gosh, am I hungry! Know what I could go for now? A great big bowl of chili!"

"*Chili?* Darling girl, you can't eat chili. Not with *your* stomach."

"Hey, the girl with the funny stomach? That's not me. That's the *old* Becky Bacall. The new one, well, she's tough. She can do anything she likes, even eat chili. She's got it all together, a cast iron stomach and the disposition of a Saint Bernard. Not only that, but she's the most confident, relaxed, together, *un*-uptight girl around. That's the *new* Becky Bacall, *me!*"

"That's my girl!" he said, and she grinned.

She followed him into the house, dropping the suitcase in the hallway. "Well," she said, heading for the kitchen, "maybe chili *is* getting a little carried away. Maybe I'll just settle for a couple of scrambled eggs and an English muffin instead!"